GIRL GONE
MISSING

Books by Marcie R. Rendon

Murder on the Red River
Girl Gone Missing

GIRL GONE MISSING

MARCIE R. RENDON

SOHO
CRIME

First published by Cinco Puntos Press in 2019.

This edition first published in 2021 by

Soho Press, Inc.

227 W 17th Street

New York, NY 10011

Library of Congress Cataloging-in-Publication Data is available.

ISBN 978-1-64129-378-5

eISBN 978-1-64129-379-2

Printed in the United States of America

10 9 8 7 6 5 4 3 2 1

*Dedicated to Earl for the secondary
PTSD experiences & to Ray for knowing more
about 'Nam and cars than me*

GIRL GONE
MISSING

Cash pulled herself up and out of her bedroom window. Her heart beat in her ears and she shivered uncontrollably. She took off running barefoot, zigzagging across the damp ground. Her eyes darted left and right. She ran toward the plowed field, in the direction that led to town. Her foot sank into the cold, wet dirt of the furrowed field. When she tried to pull her foot up, her front leg sank into the dirt even deeper. She threw herself forward, clawing at the mud with bare hands, hearing the heavy, labored breathing of the person chasing her. Fear forced her from her body so that she was soon flying above herself. She looked back to see who was chasing her, but all she could see was a body, the face obscured in the darkness. She looked down and could see herself stretched out in the mud below, buried to her knees, arms flailing. Some of her long brown hair was tangled up in her hands as she struggled to steady herself. But the body changed abruptly: no longer her struggling, not a short, dark-haired Indian girl, but a pale, tall and bony blonde, who looked up at Cash and screamed, "Help me!"

ON THAT SUNNY NOTE, CASH crawled out of bed, got dressed and headed from Fargo to the Moorhead State campus on the other side of the Red River Bridge. She nursed a tepid cup of coffee, intended to get her through her first two classes, while she tried to shake the dream from her head.

With a one-hour break between her biology and psychology classes, Cash made a beeline for her Ranchero and retrieved her cue stick from its usual place—behind the front seat. She took off across campus to the Student Union, heading for the billiard room.

It was beet-hauling season in the Valley, and Cash was driving beet truck afternoons and evenings when her class schedule allowed. Between classes she would stop at the rec hall to practice her game.

The rec hall allowed students twenty-four-hour access to the larger tables and no fee to play with a student ID. Her game had improved considerably since starting college. Barroom pool tables tended to be shorter so as not to take up too much drinking space. But here at the rec hall, the full-size tables were always open. Apparently, Midwest farmer-type college students weren't pool sharks. They spent more time writing term papers and reading textbooks.

Cash was learning a lot at Moorhead State College. She had already found out that most girls her age considered shooting pool a sin, against their church upbringing. While Cash drank Budweiser and wore straight-legged blue jeans and a clean T-shirt under a Levi jean jacket each day, a good handful of the students preferred smoking weed to drinking. They dressed in bell-bottom jeans and sheer peasant blouses: hippie attire. They talked about making love, not war. They flashed peace signs at each other as they crossed the green campus lawn.

And then there were the college jocks, the students from small-town, conference-winning sports teams who were big-shot scholarship jocks now. They were too undersized for any professional team they might hope to be scouted for. And who knew to look for them in the Red River Valley of the North anyway?

There were also the studious kids—students who in their small towns had been picked on, teased or ostracized because they got A's in algebra without cheating, who read *Macbeth* and enjoyed it. The ones who willingly stayed after school to create potions in the under-financed science labs of the high schools ruled by the captain of the football team and his cheerleader homecoming queen.

Cash had always played 8-ball for money, but here at college she had learned how to play 9-ball against fraternity jocks who considered it the only pool game worthy of their time. It kept her in shape for the money-making games at the Casbah—her home bar—over in Fargo, on the North Dakota side of the Red River.

She removed her cue stick from the fringe leather case she had made a few years ago. She screwed the two lengths of stick together and rolled it across the green of the nine-foot table.

She chalked the tip of her cue and broke the rack. She started with the 1-ball, then went ball by ball in numerical order, attempting a bank shot for each one into an opposite corner. She frustrated herself with her failures.

She stretched her five-foot, two-inch frame over the pool table, her cue stick resting easily on the arch made between her thumb and curled pointer finger.

"Cash, there you are!" Cash's zone was broken. *Shhi . . . t*. She nicked the edge of the cue ball sending it toward the 11 but about three inches off. She slid back off the table and turned to see Sharon hopping down the three rec hall steps, her flared bell-bottoms swirling around her platform shoes. Hippie girl.

"I was looking all over for you after science class. I'm in love! Do you think he's married? Do you think he fools around if he is? Don't you just love his hair, the way he kinda swoops it back over his forehead? And his bod . . . man."

Cash leaned over and aimed at the 11-ball again. "Who are we talking about?"

"Mr. Danielson." Sharon hopped up on the tall stool, crossed her legs and opened her long sweater jacket, her braless chest visible through the sheer gauze of her Indian-style shirt. "From now on I'm sitting in the front row, just like this." She tossed her long blond hair over her shoulder. "*You* can sit in the back row close to the door all by yourself. I want to be right up front where he can see *all* of me."

"You're crazy." Cash watched the 11-ball drop

smoothly into the far-left pocket. She scanned the table looking for the 12-ball and calculated the best angle for a bank shot. "He's an old man."

"He's only thirty."

"That's half dead."

"Mary Beth said she heard from someone that some of the teachers give A's for head."

"What the heck are you talking about?" Cash stood on tiptoe to reach across the table to line up on the 12. She was also learning that college hippie chicks wanted to talk about free love, weed and ending the war in Vietnam more than anything else.

"You know, head: a blow job, go down on him."

"There are easier ways to get an A."

"Maybe for you. Do you ever study? He is so groovy." Sharon exaggerated the flip of her hair over her other shoulder.

"Thought you had a boyfriend."

"Haven't you heard? *Make love, not war.*" Sharon giggled.

"Come on, grab a cue and play against me."

"Sure, Miss Shark. That's not a game. That's just me moving the balls around the table for you." Sharon hopped off the chair and grabbed a cue from the wall as Cash racked the balls.

Once again, Cash didn't hit the balls hard enough for any of them to drop. She was going to have to spend a few sessions just practicing her first shot, she could see.

"Open table," she said to Sharon.

Sharon walked around the table. "So . . . what should I shoot?"

"Try that solid right there. Nick the edge." Cash pointed at a spot on the purple ball. "Nick it soft and it'll drop right in."

Sharon slammed the cue ball into the solid purple. The ball dropped into the pocket followed by the cue ball. "Argghhh! This is why you ran out of class? To shoot pool?"

"Yeah, I drive shift tonight. Needed a few practice games." Cash ran five stripes before miscuing. "You have solids."

Sharon aimed at the 7-ball. "Did you hear about that chick who disappeared from Dahl Hall? Kids are saying maybe she got pregnant and went home. Then someone said she hitchhiked down to the Cities, but she hasn't come back. Her parents were at the Dean's office this morning."

Cash watched Sharon get a lucky break, accidentally dropping the 7 in a side pocket.

"Nope, didn't hear that."

"That's right, you got special exemption to live off campus. I hate the dorm—curfew, no boys allowed . . ." Sharon missed her shot. "This chick was in our science class—blond, used to wear a miniskirt and sit in the front row every class? Danielson was always calling on her. She'd tilt her head and cross her legs before answering the question. His eyes were never on her face. Bet she was getting A's. Your turn."

Cash took aim at the 10. "Where's she from?"

"Who?"

"The girl who's missing, dingbat."

"Oh. Shelly?" Sharon answered as if asking Cash.

"Shelly. The town of Shelly?"

"Yeah. Why?"

"Just curious." Cash had a three-ball run and lined up to bank the fourth. She missed the shot.

"Your shot."

"Hey, Cash, you got any enemies?" Sharon asked under her breath.

"Not that I know of, why?"

Sharon rolled her eyes up toward three people—a guy and two girls—standing on the steps leading into the pool table area. They looked like they could be college students, except instead of hippie clothes they wore straight-legged jeans, T-shirts and jean jackets. Just like Cash. One of the girls had her hair in two braids that hung down the front of her jacket, the other had hers pulled back in a ponytail. The guy had messy braids, like maybe he had braided them a couple days ago and hadn't redone them yet. None of them were smiling. They were clearly looking at Cash and Sharon.

Cash lit a Marlboro. She took a long drag before she lined up on the 8-ball. Out of the corner of her eye, she saw the three of them come down the steps toward the table.

They stood watching. Finally the guy said, "Play partners? Me and her"—pointing at the girl with two braids—"against you and her."

Before Sharon got the "no" out of her mouth, Cash said, "Sure. Rack 'em up."

It was a silent game, clearly between Cash and the guy, their partners missing shots each turn. Sharon was so nervous that her cue stick shook whenever she attempted a shot. Cash played cat and mouse—not doing exactly her best but not letting him win easily either—playing just well enough to keep him convinced he was better than her but that maybe she was okay.

With one ball left and the 8-ball, he asked, "Straight 8 or last pocket?"

"Straight 8 is fine," Cash said.

His partner finally spoke. "Where you from?"

"Family's from White Earth. I live over in Fargo."

"How come we haven't seen you at any of the Indian student meetings?" asked the girl with the ponytail.

"I didn't know there were any."

"Every Friday night. At Mrs. Kills Horses."

"Potluck," said the girl with braids, missing her shot at the 8.

"Where's that?" Cash had no intention of going.

"3810 10th Avenue," the guy said. "She makes sloppy joes, so there's always something even if no one brings anything."

"And beer," said the ponytail. "If you got an ID, bring some beer."

Cash rethought going. "3810 10th Avenue?"

"Yep," said the guy, making the 8-ball and laying the cue across the table. "We're going to talk about bringing AIM up from Minneapolis."

"AIM?" It was the first time Sharon spoke since the trio had arrived.

"The American Indian Movement," answered the girl with braids, looking the blond hippie chick up and down with a frown and one eyebrow raised.

Sharon stared back at her, peace and love gone from her blue eyes.

The girl with the braids looked at Cash and said, "See you Friday."

The three turned and left the rec hall. Cash re-racked the balls. "One more game. Then I gotta go."

"My boyfriend attended an AIM meeting down in the Cities when he was there last year for the Miigwetch Mahnomen PowWow. They're pretty radical. Red Power and all."

Cash wondered how Sharon knew how to pronounce Miigwetch and Mahnomen so perfectly but didn't ask. Instead, she said, "He goes to school over at NDSU?"

"Yeah, that's where most of the North Dakota Indians go. Something about the BIA money coming out of the Aberdeen office and NDSU being cheaper than sending them to school out of the Dakotas."

Another thing Cash hadn't known before starting college: her BIA money came out of Minneapolis because she was enrolled at the White Earth Reservation, which was just about forty-five miles east from where they were standing in Moorhead, Minnesota. When Wheaton, the county sheriff in Norman County, had convinced Cash to register for school, she learned she would be attending on a BIA scholarship. Wheaton told her the Minnesota Chippewa Tribe had signed a treaty with the United States government that guaranteed higher education to tribal members who wanted it. So she may as well go, do something with her life besides farm work, he said.

"Why don't you and your boyfriend come to the meeting on Friday night? And I can meet Mr. Free Love," said Cash, breaking the rack with force. This time the 1-ball dropped in a pocket. "I've got solids."

"Sloppy joes and beer? I'll see what he says. Can't imagine he'd turn that down. Only thing sweeter would be some good smoke," said Sharon. "He liked what those AIM folks were talking about."

"Yeah?"

"Guess they started a street patrol down in the Cities. The cops were picking up Indians from Franklin Avenue at closing time, just putting them in the trunks of their car and then dumping them down by the Mississippi or beating them up. So AIM started a patrol to get folks home safely. They talk about Indians standing up for their rights. My boyfriend says they're like the Black Panthers, but Indians."

Cash had no idea what Franklin Avenue was, but from Sharon's tone she assumed it was like NP Avenue over in Fargo where all the cheap 3.2 bars were and chronics like Ol' Man Willie started and ended the day in their favorite booth. Cept up here in the F-M area, it was old white men who were chronics, not Indians.

NP avenue was also where she called home, drinking at the Casbah bar each night—or each night when it wasn't beet-hauling season. She put in about an hour at the pool table after a day in the fields, playing for free drinks and the occasional dollar or five-dollar bet before heading to her apartment down the street. The only thing she knew about AIM was a couple one-night stands she'd had with a guy she called Long Braids. He had been on his way down to Minneapolis to meet up with AIM for some protest out east when their paths had crossed up Bemidji way.

"Thought those three were coming to beat you up." Sharon interrupted her thoughts, making a straight-in shot but missing her next one. "Don't know why you all look so mean all the time."

"Hmphh," breathed out Cash. She had a four-ball run before sinking the 8. She started to unscrew her cue and put it away in its fringed leather case. "Gotta get to work."

"Are you going by your apartment? Can you drop me off in Fargo?"

"Sure."

Cash and Sharon left the Student Union and headed for Cash's Ranchero. They passed groups of students on the campus lawn, studying, flirting, protesting. *Get Out of Vietnam*. Sharon talked the whole time about Danielson, then about her boyfriend's little sister who didn't like her because she was white, then again how she thought the three Indians in the pool room were coming to beat her or Cash up. Cash half-listened. With the rest of her attention, she drove and day-dreamed along to Patsy Cline singing about *someone's kisses leaving her cold*.

"Can we find some rock and roll?" Sharon reached for the radio dial and changed the station. "Here we go—the Rolling Stones."

In Fargo, Cash stopped in front of the Maytag appliance store. Home. Sharon got out, waving as she walked west. Cash watched her go. She figured that after a bit Sharon would stick out her thumb to hitch-hike the remaining mile to NDSU.

Cash ran up the stairs to her apartment, threw her schoolbooks and notebooks on the white enamel kitchen table that served as a place for her to study and eat. She lit a match, turned the gas burner on low under the tin coffeepot that still had coffee from the morning. She went into the next room and pulled off the clothes she had worn to school and tossed them over the overstuffed chair that held her "almost" clean clothes. She grabbed a different pair of jeans off the floor and jerked them on. It was the same pair she had been wearing all week while driving beet truck. She shook out a T-shirt and flannel shirt from the floor and put those on too.

Driving beet truck wasn't as dirty as driving during combine season when chaff and wheat bits got into all the creases of your clothes and the dust coated your hair like baby powder, but the smell of the beet plant clung to your garments. Cash figured it would be Christmas before the smell washed out completely. She wore a flannel shirt because the heater didn't always work in Milt Wang's trucks.

She quickly braided her waist-length hair into one long braid and pulled on her jean jacket. She filled her red Thermos with hot coffee and opened the fridge as if there might be food in there. Two bare shelves with a half-dozen carton of eggs looked out at her. She'd have to grab a tuna sandwich at the Silver Cup.

The evening waitress was used to Cash running in and saying, "Tuna sandwich." The waitress, who wore her hair in a black beehive, must have seen her coming through the front window because she was already wrapping the sandwich in wax paper: tuna, mayonnaise and a leaf of lettuce between two slices of white Wonder Bread. She put her order in a small brown paper bag and folded it over neatly, just as Cash imagined all the wives of the men she worked with prepared their liverwurst or roast beef sandwiches, neatly wrapped in wax paper too, but with homemade chocolate cake or chocolate chip cookies thrown in. Some day, Cash might ask Beehive for a slice of chocolate cake to go with her tuna sandwich.

Cash put the Ranchero in reverse, then headed east to Highway 75 going north of Moorhead. Just as she was signaling to turn on 75, she changed her mind, decided to keep going straight east to the neighboring town of Hawley, where she turned north on Highway 9, a highway that would take her directly into the county seat of Ada. After a few miles she cruised through the small town of Felton, noticing several grain trucks lined up at the elevators. She drove a few miles farther, past the Lutheran Church that sat on the edge of Borup township. Still going north, she rounded a curve on the highway and crossed a bridge over the Wild Rice River, which was not much more than a narrow creek this late in the fall.

As she came out of the curve, she saw the county sheriff's car sitting at a gravel county crossroad. She braked to a slow crawl and pulled in alongside the tan cruiser. She rolled down her window at the same time Wheaton was rolling down his. "Funding the Thanksgiving turkey giveaway?" she asked, raising an eyebrow.

"Nah, football practice is about to get over in Borup and the Ambrose boys will be speeding into Ada. One of them is dating the head cheerleader in Ada and he tries to get there just as soon as they get out of practice. One of these days he's going to come around that curve and end up in old man Peterson's field. Figure after a couple more days of seeing me sitting here, he's going to learn to slow down a bit before taking that curve. On your way to work?"

"Yeah."

"Why you coming down 9? Aren't you driving for Milt over in Halstad?"

"Yeah."

"How's school?"

"Okay."

They sat there, quiet. Cash watched the sun dip toward the western horizon. Sheriff Wheaton watched the occasional car pass on the highway.

Cash finally spoke. "Hear anything about some girl missing from Shelly?"

"Huh? So that's why you're tracking me down."

More silence, more sky and road watching.

"Well?" asked Cash.

"You just focus on your schooling, girl. Leave the police work to me."

Cash watched the sky turn to orange, pink and purple stripes over the Red River tree line twenty-some miles west across the flat farm prairie. Almost all the fields were plowed, row after row of black dirt clods stretched for acres. To the north a corn stubble field sat unplowed, most likely being left to winter over. A green John Deere tractor, slowly pulling a plow, raised dust behind it as it traveled down a gravel road a couple of miles over.

"So where is she?" Cash finally asked. "Who is she? One of the hippie chicks at school said she's missing from our biology class."

Wheaton looked over. "You know her?"

"No. This chick just says she was in our class and now she's missing. They live in the same dorm."

"She's the oldest Tweed girl. Three younger sisters. She's in college over there to get a teaching degree."

"But she's gone."

"Yeah, I drove to Shelly Tuesday to talk to her parents after they called me. Good kid. Valedictorian. Her mom's working at the dime store in Ada to help pay her college tuition. They're heartsick. The sisters crying. Not a wild kid. Not one you'd expect to just take off and not say anything."

"Good kid, huh?"

"Why, you know something?"

"Nah, just that the hippie chick said she sits in the front of the class and flirts with the science teacher to get a good grade. Just talk. I better get to work." Cash put her arm over the back of the car seat and looked both ways down Highway 9 before backing out and heading toward Ada. In her rearview mirror, she saw Wheaton give a slight wave. She waved back before rolling up her window.

It was just on the edge of getting dark as Cash pulled into Halstad. She didn't stop in town but drove on out to Milt's farm where she exchanged her Ranchero for an International Harvester dump truck. She spent the next eight hours hauling beets back and forth from Milt's fields to the sugar beet plant just on the northern edge of Moorhead. She figured she made four trips.

Hauling beets meant driving alongside the John

Deere harvester while it topped the beets, removed the green leaves, then picked them up out of the ground and carried them on a conveyor belt to the dump truck. Once the dump truck was filled, Cash drove it to the beet plant and waited in a long line with other trucks. The trucks were weighed and the farmer's name collected, assuring that the farmer would get paid the correct amount for his crop.

Some of the drivers sat in their trucks and read the daily newspaper. Others catnapped. Cash often used the time to read her homework assignments. Tonight, her curiosity was on the Valley gossip. After her first truck was weighed, she climbed out of it and walked to where a group of other drivers was standing around shooting the bull.

"Hey, Cash, thought you were too good for us already. Too busy stud-y-ing to hang out with those of us still got shit on our shoes."

Cash laughed. "Nah. Never too good for you, Bruce." Throughout junior high and high school, she and Bruce had been regulars in the wheat fields or corn furrows drinking six-pack after six-pack, listening to the country music station piped in from Oklahoma. They would drink until the beer was gone, and neither was able to walk a straight line. But he always drove her back to whatever foster place she was calling home that month.

He was one of her boy friends, never a boyfriend. White farmers were okay with their sons drinking with an Indian girl, but dating was off-limits. She had learned from Bruce that his father beat his mother—"not that much really"—but Bruce had hoped to enlist and head to Vietnam as soon as he turned eighteen to get away from home. No one ever really seemed to leave the Valley. Sure, they might move to Moorhead or Crookston and get a job inside the sugar beet factory. Or maybe sell shoes at some shop on another small-town Main Street. But really, none of them ever left. They soon found themselves back plowing fields and driving beet truck for their dads or uncles, waiting for one or the other to die so they could take over the family farm.

For Bruce, some 4F reason kept him out of 'Nam. So here he was, standing in the chilly October air, smoking Salem cigarettes and bullshitting about who was going to win the World Series, who was knocked up and had to get married, and how that would never happen to him, followed by loud guffaws and back slaps. Soon the conversation would drift back to farming and the best fertilizer to put on the ground in the spring.

The guys were so used to Cash, who had been working with them in various farm labor jobs since she was eleven, that they didn't change their talk around her.

"Give me a cigarette, I left mine in the truck." Cash reached out a hand to Bruce. She lit up and took a deep drag and coughed. Bruce slapped her on the back. "Don't choke."

"Damn, forgot you smoke these menthols." Cash coughed but took another smaller drag anyway.

"You're going to school up in Moorhead?" Steve Boyer asked her.

"Yeah."

"Know anything about that Tweed girl that disappeared?"

"First I heard about it was today."

The men all jumped in, a chorus of baritones.

"Her folks are really worried."

"Valedictorian of her senior class."

"Remember when Connie Bakkas ran off with that carnie one year after the county fair and her dad had to go down to some place in Kansas to drag her back?"

"Knocked up."

"But this is Janet. That girl is smart."

"Got some legs on her too."

"Wahooo!"

"You wish."

Some more backslapping, puffs of cigarettes. Sips of coffee from foam cups that American Crystal had provided in the warm-up shack. But Cash could tell from the looks on their faces that they were worried. Bad things that happened in the Valley were the occasional fight, sometimes a car rollover from kids drag racing down a deserted road, someone got someone pregnant and had to get married. But a town's top student didn't just disappear.

"So what happened?" Cash asked.

Bruce answered. "I don't know. Folks say she was going to the Cities for the weekend with a friend from school—go see the big city and all. But her family doesn't know who she was going with or if she went or came back."

One of the other guys jumped in. "Last they heard from her was on Friday when she called home and said she was going and would call them on Sunday when she got back. She never called."

"They got phones in the Cities—I know that," another guy added.

"Let's go, trucks are moving."

They dumped the coffee cups and ground their

cigarettes out in the gravel. A roar of truck engines filled the night air as the engines turned over all at once. Gears were shifted into first to move the trucks a couple spaces forward. The trucks that had been weighed were in line to dump their beets on another conveyor belt that would move them to an ever-larger pile of beets waiting to be moved once again into the processing plant.

Cash dumped her truckload after another half hour and then returned to Milt's field, where she waited in line for another load and another trip back to Moorhead. And so the night went. She read her English assignment and decided she would talk with Mrs. Kills Horses about testing out of English, which she had overheard from some of the other students was possible. There had been one summer in the fields where she read the entire works of Shakespeare, two whole years before anyone else in her grade level ever heard of the guy. Diagramming sentences and reworking dangling participles had been an evening pastime in various foster homes where punishment often meant long hours isolated in a bedroom. This freshman English class was not only deadly boring, but it was also an early morning class. If she was able to test out of it, it would give her a couple more hours of free time.

She read her psych assignment, all about Freud being the father of modern psychology. When she finished her biology reading right around her midnight run into Moorhead, her mind went back to the Tweed girl. As Cash munched on her tuna sandwich, she closed her eyes and scanned her memory, searching for the girl in class. Cash always sat in the back row in every class, on whichever side of the room was closest to the door. Some of the students always sat in front. Whenever a teacher asked a question, they were the first to raise their hands. From the back of the room it was a sea of blondes. Scandinavian stock clearly dominated the educational system.

Last Thursday Cash had gotten to class early because Sharon wanted to copy the work Cash had done the night before. They sat at the back of the room. While Sharon cribbed her homework, Cash watched the other students file in, some in groups of three, some alone. The jocks with slicked-back hair and the hippies with scraggly, oily locks lying on their shoulders. Girls came in bell-bottoms or miniskirts.

Cash had uncanny recall ability. She could pull up a page in her science book in her mind's eye and reread it from memory. Likewise she could pull up a day or an event and run it across a screen in her mind as if it were happening in present time. Which is what Cash did now. In her mind, Cash watched the students from last Thursday enter the room. *Ah, there she was,* the girl who must be the Tweed girl. A tall blonde—not Twiggy model thin but well-fed farmer thin—walked into the room wearing a plaid miniskirt and a mohair sweater, a book bag slung across her shoulder. She sat in the front row, front and center. Put her bag under the chair and books on the desk. Still, with her eyes almost shut, Cash scanned the room. Nothing else to see. Sun outside the window. More students coming in. Sharon closing her notebook with a sigh of relief. Mr. Danielson came into the classroom and class started. Nothing out of the ordinary.

Now Cash knew who folks were talking about when they said *the Tweed girl.*

Cash heard the other beet truck engines around her roar to life. Stretching her short frame, she pushed in the clutch with her left foot, right foot on the brake and turned the key in the ignition. She kept the truck in first as she let it roll forward to fill the space left by the other trucks. The air smelled of river mud and sugar beets mashed under truck tires. One would think it would be a syrupy, sugary smell, but it was more like stale cabbage. This fall smell was nothing compared to the rotten egg smell that would permeate the Valley come spring when the beets, which are mostly water, unfroze and the resultant fermented water filled the runoff storage ponds at the beet plant.

Cash was done hauling by two in the morning. She fetched her Ranchero from Milt's graveled farmyard, lit only by a halogen yard light, hollered *See ya*, followed by the obligatory hand wave to the other drivers. She sped back to Fargo, where she ran a quick bath, smoked a couple of Marlboros and drank a Bud before collapsing in bed.

When she woke in the morning, she made coffee and a fried egg sandwich, which she ate on her drive to school. It took a few turns around blocks near the campus before she found a free parking spot. She grabbed her books off the seat and walked to Mrs. Kills Horses' office in the administration building.

Mrs. Kills Horses was talking on the phone, her long black braids hanging over her full breasts. Dangly turquoise earrings matched her squash blossom necklace. She waved Cash in with a hand wearing three turquoise and silver rings. "Gotta get to work," she said into the receiver before putting the handset back in the cradle. "Good morning, Renee, how are you?" Cash could see that she was dressed in a long denim skirt. With the turquoise and braids, it made Mrs. Kills Horses look all Southwestern-y.

"Good. I was wondering what I have to do to test out of my English class?"

"Only the very best students do that, Cash."

"I'm getting all A's."

"It's kinda late in the quarter to think about that."

"Well, I'm kinda thinking about it. Maybe if you just tell me who I need to talk to?"

"You would have to do it this week or it really will be too late in the quarter."

Mrs. Kills Horses leaned over her desk and made a show of shuffling papers. When Cash didn't leave, she picked up a school catalog and made a show of flipping through the pages. Cash sat in a chair and waited. "Ah, here. Professor LeRoy is chair of the English Department."

As if you didn't know.

"You would need to talk with him about testing out. His office is in Weld Hall. You should really think about this, though," she said, looking motherly at Cash. "I can call over to the department and check on your grades if you want."

Cash, who rarely smiled, smiled. If Mrs. Kills Horses had been the observant type she would have noticed the smile didn't reach Cash's eyes—another skill she was learning at college. Cash lied, "Nah, that's okay. I'll talk with my dad about it tonight." She stood up and turned to leave the office.

"Tezhi said you were going to come to the meeting on Friday night. You'll get to meet the rest of the Indian students."

"Tezhi?"

"He said he ran into you shooting pool in the rec center?"

"Oh, yeah, Tezhi."

"It's potluck. All the Indian students come. I always make sloppy joes."

"Yeah, that's what Tezhi said," Cash said, rolling the new name off her tongue.

"We're going to plan a powwow and symposium, try to bring AIM in to discuss the rights of Indian students here on campus."

"I'll see. I might have to work."

"Work? Where are you working? You know, any job has to be reported and that could affect your BIA grant monies."

Damn, thought Cash. Seemed like there was more stuff to learn about *going* to school than there was actual coursework. Thank god most farmers had no problem paying cash to their workers. Looking Mrs. Kills Horses straight in the eye, she said, "My aunt might want me to babysit. Would I have to report that?"

"Gracious, no," exclaimed Mrs. Kills Horses, her long earrings swinging with her side-to-side headshake. "Just if you are working a job, you know, like wait-ressing or something."

"I wouldn't know how to do that," Cash said. She was already out the door.

"See you Friday! Six-thirty," Mrs. Kills Horses called after her.

Cash walked quickly out of the administration building and took a big gulp of fall air. Being in the brick school buildings, sitting in the classrooms, even those with large windows where she could watch the clouds move across the sky, left Cash short of breath, edgy. She took another deep breath before heading resolutely across campus to Weld Hall.

Cash paused before knocking at the oak door of Professor LeRoy. She didn't know what to say to most of the people here on campus. They talked a lot, mostly about nothing. She was used to men who knew what kind of fertilizer to put on a corn field or whose main conversation was about when to spread manure on the plowed fields. And, always, the price of grain on the Minneapolis Grain Exchange. The men she knew spent little time talking and a lot of time working. The men here on campus, their work was to talk about books, authors, ideas. But rather than talk about the day's assigned reading material, class discussions often veered off into anti-war discussions or debates about civil rights. Cash wasn't sure what either of them had to do with her.

Just as she raised her fist to knock on the door, a short, bearded man wearing tortoise-shell glasses opened it. Cash stepped back.

"Oh, I didn't mean to scare you," Professor LeRoy said, speaking with a rapid cadence, with an accent Cash had never heard before. "Come in, come in. I saw the shadow of your feet under the door. That's how I knew you were there. I don't have you in a class. Are you a freshman? Take a seat. What can I help you with?"

Without giving Cash a chance to answer, Professor LeRoy plowed on. "Great weather we're having, isn't it? When I moved here from New York everyone told me to appreciate the fall, that the winters would be real kickers. They weren't kidding. Just a matter of time before the snow falls, right? So what can I do for you?

You want to drop your class? Switch teachers? In my experience, one teacher is as good as the next, present company exempted. Ha." He took a breath while shuffling papers on his desk from one pile to another.

In that space Cash blurted out, "I want to test out of English 101."

Professor LeRoy stopped shuffling papers mid-air and stared at her.

"I'm a straight-A student."

"College is a little different than high school. I've been teaching here for fifteen years, and the English teachers at these farm schools have barely heard of Shakespeare, let alone Tennessee Williams or Truman Capote. Even with straight A's, I don't know how you can expect to pass a college-level test without taking the course."

"I can do it."

"Who is your teacher this quarter?"

"Mr. Horace."

"You don't like him? Other students love having him. He grades on the curve. Makes it easy to pass. You don't want to get up that early, is that it?"

"I was told students had the option to test out if they wanted. I want to test out."

LeRoy shuffled more papers. Cash watched him

silently. She wondered to herself what it was about her request that was driving Mrs. Kills Horses and now Professor LeRoy crazy.

"Most of the students who make this request were the top of their high school classes."

More silence. More shuffling of papers.

Cash lit up a Marlboro. LeRoy pushed a green glass ashtray across his desk. Smoke filled the air. Some of the anxiety left Cash's chest with each exhale.

"You're a freshman?"

"Yes. Do I have to fill out some papers or something to take the test?"

"Well." He moved more papers around, pulled a drawer open and brought more papers out. "This is the form to request the test."

Cash reached for the paper. Dean LeRoy put it down on his desk. "You sure you want to do this?"

"What happens if I fail it?" Cash asked.

"You would have to continue in Mr. Horace's class. Did you talk to him about this? Does he know you want to test out?"

"No. I talked to Mrs. Kills Horses. She gave me your name and sent me over here."

"Well, I don't know that it's such a good idea, but if you have your mind set on it, I suppose you can give it a try. You can fill out the form and then schedule a time to take the test. You would have to sit in my classroom and take it. Take it under observation."

"Today?"

"No, no, no. Fill out the form, sleep on it. Come back tomorrow and let me know if you still want to do it."

Cash put out her cigarette and reached across his desk for the form. She picked a pen up off his desk and began to fill it out. LeRoy stood up and opened the window to let some of the smoke out. He sat back down and shuffled more papers. Cash pushed the filled-out form toward him. "I'll stop back tomorrow for you to tell me what day I can take the test." She turned and almost ran out of the building, taking big gulps of air.

She walked at a fast clip all the way to her Ranchero three blocks away. She jumped in, turned the key in the ignition and drove away, straight to the Casbah, her home away from home. She used the cigarette lighter to light up.

It was too early in the day for the brothers, Ole and Carl, to be there. None of the other regulars were there either, except Ol' Man Willie.

Cash realized she had never been at the bar in the

morning. She usually arrived later in the evening when Willie, more often than not, was passed out in the farthest back oak booth. This early in the morning, he was sitting up at the bar, hunched over a glass of 3.2 tap beer. He looked at Cash, tipped his glass at her and said, "Oh, what is the world coming to when the young ones show up for breakfast?" He took a big gulp.

Shorty Nelson, owner and bartender, stood behind the bar, a white towel slung over his shoulder. His shirt actually looked ironed. He looked neat and put together. Not how he normally looked at the end of the night. "What are you doing here? Aren't you s'posed to be in school?"

"Give me a Bud." Cash pushed money across the polished counter. "Those folks drive me crazy."

"You drive me crazy," Willie slurred, wrapping a gray-haired arm around Cash's waist and pulling her against his side. The smell of stale armpits mixed with morning-after beer almost made Cash gag as she pushed away and jerked out of his grasp.

"Creep!"

Willie rubbed his thigh, close to his crotch, with the hand that wasn't holding his beer glass. He grinned, yellow tobacco-stained teeth appeared beneath his

Hitler-style mustache. For a split-second Cash wondered how, in his constantly drunken state, he managed to maintain the perfect square above his upper lip, but then an involuntary shudder shook her body as she noticed the bulge in his pants, the pants still stained from last night's drunk.

"Jeezus," she said, grabbing the Bud, taking a big drink and heading to the coin-operated pool table. She dug four quarters out of her jeans pocket, put them in the coin slot and listened to the comforting sound of billiard balls dropping. She grabbed a house cue because she hadn't even thought to bring her own, rolled it across the green felt, saw that it was warped a bit, put that one back and took another. That one was a bit straighter, if a tad lighter, but it would work. She racked the balls and in one fluid movement removed the wooden triangle, seized the cue stick, leaned over the table and then sent the cue ball flying into the racked balls, causing three of them to drop into separate pockets.

Shorty leaned on his forearms across the bar, watching Cash play against herself. "You know, Cash, Willie here used to be one of the richest farmers in the Valley."

"Still am," interrupted Willie.

"Until he took to coming in here mornings. Soon he was spending more time drinking than plowing."

"I can still plow." Willie leered for Shorty's benefit, rubbing his thigh again, tipping his glass in Cash's direction before killing it off. He wiped the beer foam from his mustache with his forearm and pointed the glass at Shorty. "Another. That's why I had sons. They run the farm for me since my arthritis kicked in. They don't need a college degree to farm."

Shorty refilled his glass saying, "Just shut up and drink, old man. Cash, you got a good thing going, kid. What are you doing here instead of at class?"

Cash leaned on her cue stick. She stared hard at Shorty, willing him to shut up.

"Don't you know Ole and Carl are in here every night bragging to anyone who will listen about how you are going to college? Everyone's proud of you."

"Damn straight," said Willie, lifting his refilled glass.

"Shut up," Cash said under her breath, sending the 9-ball into a side pocket. To Shorty, she said, "I just don't know, Shorty. It's a whole different world."

"You're smart, Cash."

"I don't think smart is the issue," said Cash, lining up the cue ball on the 2-ball, sitting three inches off a corner pocket. "These folks talk a different language. Dress different. Sit inside brick buildings all day and think of fancy ways to string words together instead of just saying things plain out. Plus, I think the teachers all think I'm stupid just because I'm Indian. I'm not used to folks treating me like I'm stupid. Being mean or calling me names or being disgusting," she said, pointing her cue stick toward Willie, "that, I'm used to, but being thought of as stupid just because I'm Indian? Pisses me off." She dropped the 8-ball into the same corner as the 2. With the table cleared, she put four more quarters into the table and racked the balls.

As she broke and started shooting, she said, "And these beginner classes are dumb. I learned all this stuff in high school. I don't see why I have to take it all over again. I heard that students can test out of these baby classes, but when I asked, everyone treated me like I'm just a dumb Indian."

"Are they gonna let you though?" asked Shorty, flicking his rag across the counter again.

Cash stood up from the table and looked at him across the bar. She took a drink of her Bud and a drag of her cigarette. "I filled out the *form* to test out of English this morning," she said with heavy sarcasm. "I'm going to go talk to the chair again tomorrow to find out when he'll let me take the test." She shot a couple more balls into the table before continuing.

"Then I'll go talk to the chair of the science department about trying to test out of his class too. I can already recite the periodic table frontwards and backwards. I know photosynthesis is what makes us rich here in the Bread Basket of the World." Cash waved her cue stick and beer bottle in a wide arc. "I don't think I need to be in a classroom, getting a sore ass sitting on hard chairs, smelling some strange oil these hippies wear to cover the smell of the marijuana they smoke, just to have some old guy tell me that corn and sugar beets need sun to grow." Cash started furiously shooting balls into pockets. "If I test out, I can just take my psychology and judo classes. Classes I might actually learn something in."

"Can you do that? I mean, do they let students just test out of classes?" Shorty asked.

"That's what it says in the student handbook," answered Cash. "If I can test out, I'll be free for the rest of the quarter." She swung her cue over the pool table. "And I can get my game back. I don't think I was cut out to sit inside brick buildings."

"You're still driving truck at night, right?"

"Yeah, that's why I haven't been in to shoot. School

all day, driving truck at night. I just couldn't take it anymore this morning. At school, they have these big 9-foot tables. I go over there and play between classes, but I miss this," she said, waving her cue around the bar, taking another drink of beer and a drag of her Marlboro. "Did you hear about that girl from the college who is missing?"

Shorty wiped the bar with his rag, sopping up the beer Willie had spilled while pushing himself off the bar stool for an unsteady walk to the bathroom. At least he was making it there, not using the back booth, as was his nightly habit. All the regulars knew never to sit in that booth and newcomers soon moved because of the stench.

"Some of the folks were talking. Then there was an article in *The Forum*."

"Oh? I didn't see that."

"Yeah, just how she seems to have gone to the Cities and hasn't been heard from since. Her folks are all worried."

"She's in my science class. Was."

"Whaddya think happened?"

"I don't know. I talked to Wheaton last night. He's asking around." Cash cleared the table of all the billiard balls. "I s'pose I better go back." She returned the bar cue to an empty slot on the wall rack. "Guess I've missed my English class, but I can still make science, then this afternoon my last class is judo. Soon I'll be able to kick fools off bar stools." She pantomimed a sidekick in Willie's direction.

"Keep your nose in the books," Shorty hollered as the bar door closed behind her.

BACK AT CAMPUS, SHE LUCKED out and pulled into a parking spot just as another car left, right in front of the main buildings. She grabbed her science book and papers off the passenger seat and went to class. The stream of students passing in the halls made her feel claustrophobic. She was used to the open fields of the prairie. The crush of human bodies, people rushing with no regard for the space around them or the presence of another being, made it hard for her to breathe. She clung to the brick wall and sidled past folks in a hurry, not wanting someone else to grab her seat at the back of the class.

This classroom had old-fashioned wooden desks, leftovers from the '50s. Unlike the English Department's newer metal desks and plastic chairs, these had names and chemical formulas carved into the wood, which meant you had to write your notes on top of a book or your paper would end up with holes every time you hit a carved indent.

Mr. Danielson was at the front of the room, erasing the previous teacher's scientific equations from the chalkboard. He was wearing blue jeans with a white shirt tucked in. Close to six feet tall, he had his pale blond hair pulled back in a ponytail, loose strands escaping the rubber band. Cash supposed he looked "hot" in a Rod Stewart kinda way. He started writing notes on the board.

Sharon walked in the door, wearing a miniskirt that barely covered her hind end. She winked at Cash and then took a seat in the front row, crossing her legs seductively just as Mr. Danielson turned around from the board. Cash shook her head and opened her science book to the day's assigned page.

She had just started rereading the assignment when she heard a soft cough from Sharon. Cash looked toward Sharon. Cash could tell from the way Sharon was leaning back grinning at her that she was sitting with her legs sprawled wide open. When Sharon caught Cash's eye, Sharon laughed and sat up straight. Mr. Danielson turned around at the laugh, looking at Sharon, who turned back to look at Cash again. When she did, Mr. Danielson followed her eyes to the back of the room. *Damn*, thought Cash, dipping her head downward, pretending to read from the book.

The classroom filled. For the next forty minutes, Mr. Danielson expounded on the virtues of photosynthesis, all the while talking about the hibiscus plant and trees in the rain forest. It wasn't until he briefly mentioned that algae also use photosynthesis that Cash wrote in her notebook—horse tanks.

Cash was more intrigued by the interplay of personalities happening at the front of the room anyways. Sharon would raise her hand and ask a random, useless question. When Mr. Danielson looked at her to respond, Sharon would posture in ways that sent a signal to everyone in the class that she was flirting with him. Her antics weren't lost on Mr. Danielson. He stood a little straighter when answering her. By the end of the class, he was sitting on the large wooden desk facing the students, his long legs, in blue jeans, stretched out in front of him, feet crossed at the ankles, while he and Sharon talked about whether or not plants needed photosynthesis to reproduce. No one was taking notes. They were all watching the not-at-all-subtle dance happening between teacher and student. When one of the male students slammed his textbook shut, some kids in the class jumped. They all looked at the clock and started shifting out of their chairs, getting their belongings together as Mr. Danielson stood up quickly and said, "Read chapter seven, pages 212 to 245. There will be a test tomorrow. See you all then."

Cash was walking out the door when Sharon called her back. Cash turned. Sharon was standing by the desk with Mr. Danielson standing right next to her. "Cash, do you have a piece of paper I can borrow—to write down tomorrow's assignment on?" Sharon asked with wide-eyed innocence.

Cash almost kept on walking, but Mr. Danielson said, "Cash. I haven't seen that name on the class roster. Is that a nickname?"

Cash took a step back into the room and looked up at him. He was looking at her the way she had seen farmers look at livestock—curious, interested, assessing the livestock's temperament, determining how easy they could be led into the chute that got them on the truck to take to the slaughter market. Cash shivered, pulling her books close across her chest.

Sharon answered for her. "She just goes by Cash. Her real name is Renee. Do you have a piece of paper?" she asked again.

Without moving farther into the room, Cash set her

books down on the closest desk and ripped a piece of paper out of her notebook. She held it out at arm's length so Sharon had to walk toward her to get it. "Come on, let's go." Cash looked hard into Sharon's eyes as Sharon took the paper. "Come on."

"I have to get the assignment," said Sharon, smiling stupidly.

"Looks like you have gotten all A's on your quizzes so far, Renee. Renee Blackbear?" said Mr. Danielson, looking through his grade book.

Cash stayed where she was, close to the door. The thought flashed through her mind that maybe it would be a really good idea to test out of this class for more reasons than just not having to sit through it. Cash stood silent as Sharon walked back toward Mr. Danielson, her hips swinging under her miniskirt. When she bent over the desk to write, the skirt rode up indecently. The move was not lost on Mr. Danielson. "Sharon, let's go," said Cash.

"Do you offer a way to get extra credit for those of us who don't quite understand the sciences?" asked Sharon, finally standing up and tucking her pencil behind her ear. A couple students entered the classroom, jostling past Cash who was still standing by the doorway.

"You could stop by my office at the end of the day,"

he answered Sharon with a smile that made Cash want to gag. "I have a class in here in three minutes." He gestured toward the students filing in.

Sharon turned toward Cash, hips still swinging. At the same time, a slender blonde approached the teacher. He turned his full attention, the attention he had just poured out on Sharon, on the blonde, who laughed and smiled hello to him.

In the hallway, Cash said, "Are you out of your mind? That guy's a total creep."

"No, he's not. He's hot."

"Drop it, Sharon."

"I'm going to see what kind of 'extra credit' he offers."

"Don't."

"Come on, don't be such a fuddy-duddy." Sharon was almost skipping down the flight of stairs that would take them out of the building. "I'm in looooove!"

"You already have a boyfriend. Don't be stupid. He's old enough to be your dad."

"He is not!"

Cash pushed open the door to the outside. "He's a creep."

"Renee! Renee!" A male voice called out behind them as they reached the bottom step outside the science building.

Sharon turned around, almost tripping. She whispered, "He's calling you!"

"Huh?"

"Renee."

Mr. Danielson was standing right behind them. He held her notebook in his hand. "You left this on a desk. You might need your notes for the quiz tomorrow. If you wanted to stop by the office sometime . . . even A students can use extra credit. Gotta get back to the classroom." He sprinted back up the stairs. "See you later this afternoon, Sharon," he called back.

Cash looked at Sharon and said firmly, "He *is* a creep. Stay away from him and his stupid extra credit." Sharon pouted until they parted company midway across campus.

Cash went to judo. Self-defense was a priority after she had been grabbed twice earlier in the fall. The first time was by the Day Dodge kids up on the Red Lake Reservation where she had gone to help after their dad was murdered and their mom died. The second was when the guys who had killed their dad had nabbed her off the main street of Halstad and threatened to kill her. Though Cash traveled with a .22 rifle, she felt she needed some maneuvering skills. Both times she'd been nabbed, her rifle was tucked behind the seat of her Ranchero.

After judo class, she grabbed a tuna sandwich at the Silver Cup and then headed north out of town to spend another night driving beet truck.

The evening was dull until Jim Jenson climbed into the cab of her truck while she was waiting to dump a load of beets. Jim was wearing a plaid wool shirt, his thermal undershirt visible at the neck, and the standard farmer blue jeans. Grinning, he slid across the cracked leather seat of the International Harvester truck and nuzzled her neck. "Where you been, Cash? I need me some Cash." The hair on the nape of her neck tickled.

"Ahh, get away," she said, pushing against his skinny chest. "Stop—that gives me the shivers."

"Where you been? You're never at the Casbah anymore. And your door has been locked every time I've come up to your place. You never used to lock me out. What's going on?"

"I gotta get up and get to school." She tapped the book on the seat between them. "Drive truck half the night, sleep a bit, and then I gotta get to school."

Jim kept his arm across her shoulders, pulling her into him. "Haven't seen you since we lost that pool tournament at the Flame. You still mad at me about that?"

"We? Don't count me in on that. You lost that one all yourself."

"Come on, Cash, don't be so hard on me. I miss you."

His hand slid up her leg.

"Go on." She pushed away again. "I have to study. I got a quiz tomorrow in science I gotta study for."

Jim backed off and slid over to the passenger side of the truck. His grin was gone. He gazed out the window then back to Cash. "You gonna come to the Casbah this weekend?"

Cash looked at him. She and Jim were pool partners. Had been "sleep together" partners until a month ago, when he had lost a pool tournament that cost her her rent money. Cash had been pretty drunk and had gotten 86'd from the Flame when she had upturned a couple of tables on her way out of the bar. She'd also cleared a few with her other arm, busting glass all over. All because the barmaid had accused her of hiding beer in her purse at closing time.

Cash had never carried a purse. She had tucked two bottles into the back of her jeans, but that wasn't a purse. Cash looked at Jim. He was built thin, hair slicked back, his farmer tan from the summer fading. His Scandinavian whiteness would be fully back by Thanksgiving. He was looking at her with a hopeful grin. "Why'd you go crazy that night anyways? Not the first time we lost."

Cash started to laugh in spite of herself. "I don't know. She just pissed me off. Only white girls carry purses. Maybe if she'd just accused me of taking the beers, I woulda put them on the table. But it was the purse that got me."

Cash laughed harder.

"You're crazy."

Cash looked at him. He was smiling. That smile reminded her that earlier in the day of the lost pool tournament she had seen Jim and his wife and kids at a restaurant in the new mall west of town. The smile he had now was the same happy smile he had had that day eating with his family. Cash quickly looked away.

"What?"

"Nothin'."

"Criminy, one minute you're laughing like crazy and the next you're looking at me like you want to kill me."

Cash took a drink of lukewarm coffee from her Thermos. "I'm just tired, Jim. School. Work. I'm just getting used to school."

"Let me come over after we're done with the shift here. I'll just stay for a minute."

"That wouldn't be much fun." Cash grinned.

The truck ahead of them was moving forward. Jim opened the passenger door. As he hopped down, he said, "Leave the door open, okay?"

"Okay, for a minute." Cash laughed.

Cash watched him in the side mirror as he walked back to his truck. He told her he was married before they ever slept together. Mostly he would come to her apartment after a night of drinking and shooting pool. They would have sex and he would leave. The wife and kids he told her about weren't real to her until that afternoon when Cash saw them as a family.

Cash finished her shift, retrieved her Ranchero and drove back into Fargo. Out of habit, she drove by the Casbah even though it was a couple of hours past closing time. The bar was dark except for the neon light of the Hamm's beer sign, which hung above the bar inside, shining through the window. Back at her apartment, she took a quick bath, grabbed a Bud from the fridge and crawled into bed. Halfway through the bottle, Jim arrived, stayed a bit longer than a minute, and then headed northwest out of town to his wife and kids. Cash was asleep before he pulled the door shut and locked it after himself.

Cash pulled herself up and out of her bedroom window. Fear propelled her, running barefoot, across the damp ground, listening to heavy breathing gaining on her. She ran toward the plowed field ahead, heading to town. Her foot sank into the cold dirt of the furrowed field. When she tried to pull her foot up, her front leg sank farther into the dirt. She threw herself forward, clawing with bare hands, her waist-length dark brown hair caught in her hurried grasps. She could still hear the heavy, labored breathing of the person chasing her. Fear forced her from her body so she was soon flying above herself. Looking down she saw herself stretched out in the mud below, buried to her knees, arms flailing. Cash circled in the air above like a bird of prey looking down at a mouse in the field. She tried to see who was chasing her, but the face was obscured in the darkness. Below, her own body changed to a paler, longer-legged, long-haired blonde. The young woman looked up at Cash and screamed, "Help me!"

CASH SAT STRAIGHT UP IN bed, then thudded back onto her pillow. Her heart was racing. The same dream, two nights in a row. *Damn.* She glanced over at the clock sitting on the dresser; the hands read 3:40. Cash reached over and flipped on the lamp, swung her legs over the edge of the bed and reached around until she found the half-finished bottle of Bud on the floor. She killed it, lay back down without turning off the light, flipped over the pillow and fluffed it up under her head.

She ran the dream back through her mind. She remembered, in foster homes, having that dream as a recurring nightmare. When she flew out of her body and looked back at who was chasing her, it was always a foster parent. In those dreams, when she got stuck in the mud of the field and took off, up and out of her body and started flying, she eventually looked down.

When she saw herself, she reached down and pulled herself up, out of the field and into the sky. But in this dream, when she looked down she saw another body there instead of hers. It creeped her out. She flipped the pillow again and this time folded it in half with her head stuck inside.

She needed to sleep. She planned to go ask the chair of science about testing out of biology and, if she was lucky, Professor LeRoy from the English Department would let her take that test tomorrow. She started counting backward from ten. Ten, nine, eight and on to one. Then she started counting forward. She almost always fell back asleep before she reached fifty and tonight was no different.

She woke again at seven when the alarm went off. She brushed her hair, quickly braided it into one braid down the center of her back and washed her face while her coffee was brewing. She rinsed out her Thermos before filling it with hot coffee, made a fried egg sandwich, grabbed her book and notebooks off the kitchen table and headed to school.

The first place she stopped was LeRoy's office.

"Oh," he said, leaning back in his chair as she entered. "I looked up your grades. Not bad. You did all right in high school too, I see."

Cash stood waiting.

"So . . . you still want to test out?"

"Yes."

"All right . . . if you're sure. Come back here, not *here*, but to Room 103 in this building at two. Can you come at two?"

Cash nodded her head yes.

"All right. Come back at two, Room 103, and we'll see how you do. Bring a couple of pencils, sharpened, to write with. Most of it is multiple choice, but you'll also have to write an essay."

He raised his eyebrows. "Is an essay going to be too hard?"

Cash shook her head and turned to leave.

"It's early enough in the quarter, if you pass, you could register for the next level English," LeRoy said to her back.

Cash hadn't thought about that. Wasn't ready to think about that. "I'll think about it," she said as she closed the door shut behind her.

Maybe she could do this school thing without taking any classes, she thought as she walked through the English building, her footsteps along with the voices of other students echoing off the hardwood floor.

AFTER SHE SAT THROUGH WHAT she hoped was her last boring English 101 class, she stepped out into the fall air and fought the urge to keep walking right to her Ranchero, to drive north along the river . . . or go to the Casbah . . . or go eat. To do anything but go to science class and take that stupid test. Instead, she walked across the Commons and entered the science building, trudged up the stairs to the second floor.

Sharon was already there, sitting front and center, wearing a different miniskirt than she had worn the day before. This one had fake fringe leather on the hem. Sharon leered at Mr. Danielson's back as he wrote notes on the blackboard.

Cash took her usual spot at the back of the room. She was done with the test way before most of the other students. Mr. Danielson had said they could leave once they were finished. But, rather than call attention to herself by being the first one up, Cash pretended to keep working while looking around the room at the other students. Her mind drifted to her dream of the blonde screaming for help, the blonde who just a week ago sat at the front of the room where Sharon now sat. Thinking about the dream raised the hair on the back of her neck.

Cash caught Mr. Danielson staring at her. She

ducked her head and pretended to write more on the test. Finally two guys got up and turned their tests in. *Thank god.* A few seconds later, Cash gathered her books and papers, dropped her test on Danielson's desk and walked out of the room, down the stairs into the fresh air. She shivered, and not from the cold. Danielson gave her the creeps.

She remembered she was going to ask Chairman Olsen of the Science Department about testing out too. She went back in the building, found his door and walked through the same conversation she'd had earlier with the chair of the English Department. The Science chair was less verbal. He looked at her through horn-rimmed glasses. He had a pencil stuck behind his left ear. He mumbled, "Sure, come in on Friday at noon."

Cash nodded and got the heck out of his room. It reeked of formaldehyde.

She was halfway across the Commons on her way to the rec hall when Sharon caught up with her. She babbled on for the next hour, over the sound of pool balls dropping, about how groovy Mr. Danielson was. After forty minutes, Cash cleared the table one last time, and told Sharon to "get over it."

At the end of the hour she went to her psych class.

The information in this class was new to her. She found the reading and homework easy, but she didn't think it would make sense to try to test out of it.

After psych, she went to judo in the school gym. She threw and got thrown for an hour. At the end, she was breathing hard, exhausted. She was going to have to start exercising like she used to in high school. Without working in the fields full time, she could tell she was losing muscle.

Right at two, Cash returned to Room 103 in the English building. The class was in progress, but when LeRoy saw her looking in the door window, he motioned for her to come in. He handed her some standardized test pages and a few pages of lined blank paper. "Your essay should be a comparative essay on Shakespeare and a twentieth-century poet or writer. There's a desk at the back you can sit at. Just bring it all up here when you're finished."

Cash was done with the multiple-choice test a few minutes shy of fifteen. She sat and stared out the classroom window for another ten. There was a maple tree, its leaves brilliant fall red. A small bird, a wren, hopped from branch to branch. Cash thought about the line from Shakespeare's *Julius Caesar*—"Et tu, Brute?"—and how many times she had been betrayed, or felt betrayed, by families who swore to the social workers' faces, faces that were either lined with worry or a churchy cheerfulness, that they would care for her. She thought about Langston Hughes' poem, *Dream Variations*. Before she gave up hope, she had dreamed of a day when she could whirl and dance in the sun. She was startled out of her reverie by LeRoy blocking out the window.

"You going to be able to finish?"

"Of course," answered Cash. She grabbed her pencil. For the next twenty-five minutes, she wrote without stopping. When the bell rang, she put a period on the last sentence and wrote her name at the top of each page. She handed them to LeRoy and walked out of the room, making a beeline for the door. Outside she shook the tension from her shoulders and looked to the red maple where the wren continued its hopping.

Mission accomplished.

Cash drove through the town of Moorhead. Lawns were turning brown. Orange and yellow leaves were falling from the trees. It wasn't winter cold yet, but the fall chill was in the air. She stopped at the red light on Main and lit up a Marlboro waiting for the light to change. Station wagons passed by, driven by farm wives in town for doctor's appointments or grocery shopping. Ford pickup trucks pulling broken farm equipment dropped chunks of field dirt on the pavement on their way to the implement shop. On the radio, Merle Haggard turned *twenty-one in prison while his mama cried*. For a fleeting second, Cash wondered about her own mom, but she quickly shut that door in her mind. She took another drag of her cigarette and turned up the volume on the radio.

Back at her apartment, she put the tuna sandwich she had gotten at the Silver Cup in her lunch box with a full Thermos of coffee. She changed into work clothes and headed north along the river.

As she neared Perley, she could see Wheaton's cruiser sitting in the graveled parking lot of the town's grain elevators. As she got closer, Wheaton flashed his headlights at her. She pulled in alongside his car, driver window to driver window.

"How's school?"

"Okay."

"Passing?"

"Of course." Smoke from her cigarette filled the air between them.

"Have you heard anything more about the Tweed girl?"

"Nah. Nothing more than last time we talked. Folks

just speculating on where she is, who she might have run off with."

"Her folks are mighty concerned. Say she never would have just run off."

Wheaton's big hands twisted nervously around the cruiser's steering wheel. "I know you're busy with school and all and driving beet truck, but I was wondering if you'd have a couple minutes to run up to their farm in Shelly with me and see if you can pick up anything that might be useful. Mind you, I wouldn't want you to say anything to her folks, just go up there with me, get a sense of them."

He watched a car on the highway speed past. They tapped on the brakes when the driver saw Wheaton's car. Wheaton flipped on the police flashers. The car on the highway slowed even more. "Maybe they'll think twice next time."

Cash flipped her cigarette out onto the gravel. *Help me*, echoed in her mind from her dream. "Okay," she answered. "Follow me to Wang's so I can leave my truck there and ride with you. You can drop me back at startin' time?"

Wheaton turned on his car. "See you there."

As he started to roll up his window, a little black dog popped its head up in the back seat.

"What is that?"

"Oh, him," said Wheaton.

"I didn't know you had a dog."

"I didn't. But I was out driving the other evening by the old Johannsson farm. I was just driving, you know, and I saw this gunnysack moving down the road."

"Gunnysack?"

"Gunnysack. First I thought the wind was blowing it. But there wasn't any wind—the sack was moving itself down the road. I pulled over and walked up to it, I could hear this pitiful whining. It was tied shut with twine. I thought maybe it was a bag of kittens that someone was trying to get rid of, but when I untied the bag this little guy was in there. Scrawny, must have been the runt of the litter that someone threw out and left for dead. Now he won't leave my side."

Wheaton looked over his shoulder at the puppy. Wheaton was a big guy. He filled the front seat, his build like an ex-football player. He kept his hair cut military short and more often than not his face was stern, the face of a cop who knew he had to mean business. But when he looked at the pup his whole face softened.

"Kinda cute—for a runt. What'd you name him?"

"Gunner." The little dog perked his ears up. "Gunny-sack is too long a name."

"Now you have a full-time deputy to ride with you," Cash said, shaking her head in amusement. "I'll meet you at the farmstead."

She pulled out, spinning gravel just for the heck of it and took off about twenty miles per hour over the speed limit for five miles before dropping down to the posted limit. She looked in the rearview mirror and saw Wheaton cruising up behind her.

As long as she'd known him, he'd never had a wife or kids or a pet. Once she dared to ask him if he was married. He brushed off the question with a quick no and moved on to another subject.

At the farmstead she hopped out of the Ranchero and got into the cruiser. Gunner jumped over the front seat and sat straight up between Wheaton and her, giving a low throat growl in Cash's direction.

"Look at him," she said. "He's protecting you from me."

Wheaton scratched the pup behind the ears. "Enough, Gunner. She's okay." The dog laid its head on Wheaton's leg.

"Looks like a mix between a black lab and a shep-herd, you think?"

"Yeah, that's kinda what I thought too."

Wheaton put the cruiser in gear and headed out of the farm and down the county road. Cash caught the pup's eye. He gave another growl.

"You better get used to me, mutt. I knew Wheaton long before you." She turned to Wheaton and asked, "What's with you and strays on gravel roads? You picked me outta the ditch when I was a kid. Haven't seen my mom since she rolled the car there, but somehow I have the law on my side. Not complaining, mind you, but . . ." She looked down at the pup. "And now here's this guy. How could someone just put 'em in a gunnysack and leave 'em for dead?"

"You know, folks do it all the time with cats. They want cats to keep the rats and mice out of the barns and grain bins, but after a few generations you can end up with twenty feral cats. Ain't nothing to find a bag of them thrown in the river or down at the county dump. But this little guy, someone just threw him out like trash. He must have wanted to live, running down the road inside a gunnysack." The pup laid its head back down on Wheaton's lap.

Wheaton turned the car north on the paved highway going toward Shelly, a small town north of the county seat. Like all the other small towns around, the actual town's population was under two hundred. It had one main street and it was the highway they were driving on. The prairie was so flat Cash could see the water tower seven miles out.

"Where's their farm?"

"Just a couple miles north of town, then east a quarter of a mile. Told them we'd get there about four-thirty."

Wheaton checked his watch. They rode the last seven miles into town in an easy silence. Cash looked out her window at the fields that had been plowed under for the season. Corn and wheat, alfalfa and barley all harvested and either on trains to the Twin Cities or stored in barns and grain bins throughout the Valley. The only fields where men were still working were the beet fields. Even now, machines were out in the fields picking the beets. And trucks that only a month ago had been following combines around a wheat field were now loaded down and piled high with the gray-colored sugar beets, all headed south to the sugar beet plant.

Beet season took a toll on the county roads that the other crops didn't. The truckload of beets weighed a lot more than corn or wheat, probably because the beetroots were water dense. They also tended to have field dirt clinging to them even though the newer machines were better at cleaning the large clumps off the roots before they were ever loaded on the trucks. As a result of the weight and the mud and the sheer number of trucks running night and day during beet harvest season, the county roads got torn up badly. And the paved roads developed a sheen of mud. This close to the Red River, the mud was mixed with river clay that was slicker than ice if a rainfall or early frost or, god forbid, an early snow coated the road.

They passed quickly through the small town of Shelly in the same easy silence. Main Street was bare of traffic. One lone pickup truck sat in front of the town bar. Cash felt the itch, wondering if they had a pool table. Not something Wheaton was likely to stop for. A trio of three teenagers walked down a side street. The yellow school bus that had just dropped them off was closing its door and pulling away. In towns this small, everyone knew everyone: those kids knew the Tweed girl. If not her, her brothers and sisters. Maybe they all went to the same church or 4-H club.

Wheaton sped up as they reached the town's edge. Within minutes he was pulling into a farmyard. The house was an older two-story farmhouse, not one of the ranch-style houses some of the better-to-do farmers were having built. Their wives had grown tired of living in the "old" farmstead house, which had been built when the farms were first homesteaded in this area. Over the years, rooms were added on. Indoor plumbing was installed. Attics were turned into bedrooms as the family had more children.

Cash had lived in a few houses like that during her time in foster care. Once her room was a lean-to porch that was hotter than hell in summer and freezing cold in winter, while the social worker was made to believe she slept upstairs with the oldest daughter. In another home, her room was in a musty basement, the walls of fieldstone always damp to the touch. Cash hadn't stayed there too long. Just long enough to be nursemaid to the foster mother after she gave birth to her seventh child. An ugly squalling bald lump of flour dough is how Cash had thought of the newborn.

A ginger-colored collie mix ran up to the cruiser. Gunner jumped on Wheaton's lap growling furiously, the black fur on his neck standing straight up.

"Calm down, Gunner. Calm down. Get in back. Everything's okay. Stay."

Wheaton and Cash got out of the car. A man in work overalls and a blue shirt stood holding the door open, waiting for them to reach him. His blond hair hung over his furrowed forehead. His shoulders slumped. He wasn't that old, probably not even forty, but he'd become an old man in the time since his daughter had disappeared. He didn't say a word when Wheaton and Cash got to the door, just held it open and gestured with his hand to go on in.

Right inside the doorway, work clothes and jackets hung on farmer nails pounded into the wall. Work boots and shoes sat in a tidy row on a linoleum floor, right off the edge of a braided rag rug.

Mr. Tweed walked them to the round oak table in the kitchen with seven wooden chairs around it. He pulled one out for each of them. Cash looked around the room. Stove and fridge along one side. Kitchen sink underneath a window facing the driveway into the farmyard. Homemade curtains hung from the window. Tweed's wife placed two ceramic mugs of hot coffee in front of them. Her shaking hands caused some coffee to spill on the table in front of Cash. "Sorry," she mumbled as she turned and walked back to the kitchen counter.

She was tall and bony, wearing a yellow cotton dress printed with small violet flowers. Cash could see she'd sewn it herself.

She recognized the pattern from one she had seen

in the Life section of the *Fargo Forum* a few months before. Each Sunday the paper ran a picture of a sewing pattern women could mail order. When the pattern arrived, wives would go shop for fabric at JCPenney or the larger fabric store in Moorhead.

Mrs. Tweed had clearly taken pride in sewing the dress. The dress was topstitched in all the right places and even had front pockets with buttons sewn on. Judging by the wrinkles and food stains on the sides of the dress, Cash figured she'd been wearing it for a few days straight. Her home-permed hair was pulled back with a rubber band. Loose strands hung limply around her sorrowful face. She grabbed a dishrag from the sink and another cup of coffee for her husband. She wiped up the small spill in front of Cash and sat down heavily on a wooden chair by her husband, damp dishrag still in her hand. He put his hand on her arm as if to assure her things were fine, though neither of them believed it.

"This is Renee Blackbear. Folks around here call her Cash. Sometimes she works with me, but right now she's going to school up in Moorhead."

"You're the one who almost got burned up by the men that killed the man from Red Lake, aren't you?" Mrs. Tweed leaned forward anxiously. "Do you know

Janet?" she asked before Cash could answer yes to the first question.

Cash shook her head no. "We're in the same science class. I don't know her though. She sits in front. I sit in back." Cash took a sip of the strong black coffee.

"I'm wondering if there's anything new you've thought of since I was last out," Wheaton spoke in Mr. Tweed's direction.

Mr. Tweed tightened his lips. "No, nothing. I don't know where she went. Why would she go anywhere? She said she was going to the Cities with some friends. We told her not to go, didn't we, Ma? But she was always strongheaded. Hard enough having her go off to school. She didn't have any business in the Cities. But Ma here, she's the one that finally said go ahead and go. See the world. Nothin' but hard work on a farm for a woman."

His head was hung over his coffee cup, resting on the palms of his hands held up by his elbows.

As he rambled on, his wife started to cry, tears running from her blue eyes down her reddened cheeks. Mr. Tweed looked up and saw Wheaton and Cash looking at his wife.

"Oh, Barb, I didn't mean nothing by that. I'm always putting my big foot in my mouth. It's not your fault she went. I didn't mean it like that." He put his arm around her shoulders, as if they were just starting to date instead of a few years short of their silver wedding anniversary. He patted her shoulder. "It's not your fault."

"Maybe you could show me her room." Standing up, Cash spoke to Mrs. Tweed.

Mrs. Tweed wiped her eyes. "Sure."

Cash followed her through the living room, their footsteps deadened on the hardwood floor as they crossed a room-sized braided rug. Mrs. Tweed opened an oak door leading to a narrow wooden staircase. "She slept upstairs. Bob fixed up the attic for her when she went to high school." She chattered breathlessly as she led Cash upstairs. "Girls need more privacy than boys. Steve has a room down off the sun porch. He's starting for the A-team in football this year. Sophomore. Running back."

At the top of the stairs was another linoleum floor. Sears must have had a sale on this particular pattern because it was a match for the entryway downstairs. A double bed with a handmade quilt sat under a narrow attic window. Two pillows with matching embroidered pillowcases lay side by side at the head of the bed. A curtain rod hung from the rafters, filled with cotton dresses, some summer shifts, others darker wool blends suited for Minnesota winters. A six-drawer dresser held a cheerleading trophy from a couple years back. It was a clean and tidy room. Nothing out of place.

Mrs. Tweed stared at Cash, her hands twisting the fabric inside the pockets of her dress. "Do you ever take off on your parents like this?" she asked.

Cash looked at her. She paused before shaking her head slowly. "No."

"Are you working for the county now?"

"No. Wheaton just likes to get my opinion some-times. Do you mind if I look at her clothes?" She gestured at the clothes hanging on the metal rod.

"Go ahead."

Cash leafed through the dresses as if they were pages of a book. Images flashed through her mind as she touched each one: A classroom full of laughing kids. A dance at the Legion Hall. A church choir singing loudly. She touched a soft blue wool sweater—goose bumps ran up her arm. She shivered and saw a girl floating over a dirt field calling, "Help me."

"It gets a might cold up here now that fall is set-tling in." Mrs. Tweed must have seen Cash tremble. She sat on the bed, the metal bedsprings creaking with her weight.

"Yeah. When's the last time Janet wore this sweater?"

"I think she wore it to the college football game. That was just a couple weeks ago. Seems a lifetime now. Her grandma gave it to her as a going-away-to-college present. She didn't wear it that much. It's wool but it was chilly out that night. She was all giggly and happy. Some big date, I guess. I never dated anyone but Bob. You girls are living in different times. I just don't know." She started sobbing again.

"We can go back downstairs," Cash said. "It is chilly up here."

Mrs. Tweed leaned over and took the hem of her skirt and wiped her face. She stood up and led the way downstairs.

Mr. Tweed and Wheaton were sitting silently at the kitchen table, half-empty coffee cups in front of them. Wheaton raised his eyebrows as Cash walked into the kitchen. She nodded—she was ready to go.

"I'm sorry I don't have any more information at this time. We'll keep looking for her," said Wheaton.

Mr. Tweed stood and reached out to shake Wheaton's hand. "The hardest part is the gossip. Folks saying she ran off like that Bakkas girl did with the fair carnies a few years back. My girl isn't like that."

"Of course not. We'll keep looking."

The collie followed them to the cruiser. Gunner

peered out the driver's window and growled. "Get in back," Wheaton said.

"Got yourself a police dog like a big city policeman."

"Huh." Wheaton reached back and patted the dog's head. "Lay down."

"Did her dad say anything new?"

"No."

"Neither did her mom. Seems like something happened a couple weekends ago at the football game."

"Like what?"

Cash shrugged. "I'll ask around and see what the talk is."

They rode in silence back to the Wangs. Halfway there Gunner jumped from the backseat to the front and laid his head on Wheaton's lap. Wheaton patted the dog's shoulder. Cash watched the whole thing out of the corner of her eye. She had never seen Wheaton look so content. A dog suited him.

Once they arrived at the farm, Cash hopped out. "I'll be in touch. Gotta run get in line with a truck."

FOR THE REST OF THE week Cash drove beet truck till 2 A.M. It was slow going from the field to the beet plant, the truck heavy with tons of beets. The drive, the wait in line, gave her hours to think about the missing Tweed girl. The only thing clear to Cash was that there was a blond girl who was alive enough to call out to her for help across the time of dream space. Each night she would fall into bed dreading her dream time being as busy as her work time.

SHE LIFTED THE LEVER OF *the truck's hydraulic system and heard the steady* thump-thump *of fat sugar beets falling onto the conveyor belt that carried them into the factory. Cash felt the truck start to float as the thumping got louder and louder and took on the rhythm of "shave and a haircut, two bits."*

Cash sat up quickly in bed. She glanced out a crack in the curtain hanging over the bedroom window. It was still night out. She threw off the sheet and pulled on jeans and a T-shirt from the floor. It couldn't be Jim knocking like that. He would knock softly. If she didn't answer right away, he would creep back down the wooden stairs and go home.

The knocking started again. Cash walked to the kitchen door without turning on any lights. Outside the door, silhouetted in dim light from the streetlights, stood a guy wearing an army fatigue jacket.

"Renee?" he said loudly, hand mid-knock. "Renee Blackbear?"

Cash opened the inside door but not the screen door.

"Yeah?"

"Open the door for your brother, why don'tcha?"

"Huh?"

"Renee, it's me, your brother, let me in."

Cash's heart was beating louder than the knocking. She looked out into the street. It seemed solid. She looked at the kitchen table. It looked solid too. She reached over and touched the back of the wooden chair she always sat on. It was solid.

She reached across her body and squeezed her left bicep with her right hand. Bare seconds passed while she checked reality, making sure she wasn't dreaming.

She pushed the screen door outward. The guy in the army fatigue jacket stepped into her kitchen. He set a green duffle bag down on the floor. Cash pulled the string above the kitchen table to turn on the overhead light. She walked back to bed in the living room and looked at the clock. It was 6 A.M. She had set her alarm to go off at eight so she could make it to her eight-thirty class. She stood there, her back to the kitchen, her heart beating, her chest tight, wondering if she was going to pass out. She took a deep breath and turned and walked into the kitchen again without really looking at this guy who said he was her brother.

He had pulled out a chair and was sitting at the table watching her as she prepared coffee. All the while she looked at him out of her peripheral vision.

He wasn't very tall. His black hair was cut military short. Lean. Sinewy is the word that came to her mind. Brown skin, scarred knuckles. His brown eyes, distant but lively, jumped around her apartment—watching her, checking out her space. He lit a filterless cigarette from a pack of Camels. With the first puff he blew smoke rings over the table. Cash stood at the stove, waiting, watching for the coffee to boil, still checking him out. Her chest was steel-trap tight but her heart had slowed a bit.

She watched small bubbles form, steam rise from the top of the coffeepot, her hand at the ready on the stove knob to turn the flame down when the water reached a hard boil. She caught it right on time, turned the heat to low without any of the grounds rolling over the top of the pot. With the coffee simmering, she rotated around, reached into the open cupboard behind her and took out two thick white ceramic coffee mugs. If she remembered right, she had two cups, both from the Silver Cup Diner, carried out absentmindedly at one time or another.

She put one cup down in front of the Army guy and the other down for herself. She hesitated, unsure what to do next: he was sitting in the chair she always sat in. She finally sat down opposite him.

He blew on the cup of steaming coffee before taking a cautious sip. "Best coffee I've had since getting state-side. S'pose you're wondering how I found you?" He lit another cigarette. Cash thought she smoked a lot but this guy was chain-smoking, lighting one cigarette off the butt of the other one. "I got back a couple weeks ago. Got kicked outta the family that adopted me. Went and fought to keep America safe. Became a man! Came home and the first time I got drunk, they kicked me out. Told me to never come back. Been doing that old man's shit work since I was eight years old. Goddamn adopted me too. Told everyone in church I was their kid. *Just like one of theirs.* Shit. All my hard work is going to go to that pansy-ass kid of his, not to me, like he had me believing all those years, hoping and dreaming all them years, telling everyone I was his, just like a real son. Fuck!"

He took a big swallow of the coffee. "Ah, heck." He grinned over the coffee steam. "Easy come, easy go." He looked at her. "Damn, if you don't look just like Ma. 'Cept your hair is straight, not curly like hers was."

"She put it up in pin curls."

"That's right."

Silence.

"The people that adopted me told me you were moved from home to home and they'd heard that the sheriff had kinda taken you under his wing. I stopped by the jail in Ada and his secretary said you lived in Fargo. So I drove up here. I got me a Pontiac, a silver-gray Grand Am, with money I been saving. It's a sweet ride, sitting right out front here. Faster than a cop car."

"How'd you know where I live?"

"I stopped at a couple bars here on NP Avenue to shoot some games, drink some beer. At the Casbah the folks were talking about this Indian chick that could really shoot pool, but folks haven't seen her in a while. I told 'em I was looking for my sister, and one of the guys—think his name was Jim—said the pool shooter didn't have no family, or that the family had all been killed in a car crash years ago. Said he thought your real name was Renee. That got me thinking, maybe it was you. But we aren't all dead."

"No?"

"Hell no. Like I said, I was adopted by the farmer up by Crookston. Chi-chi, our sister, I heard she was adopted by some family out in Delaware or some shit."

Cash felt her chest tighten. A blackness formed in the pit of her stomach and began to move slowly up to her diaphragm.

"Hey!" The Army guy jumped out of his chair, pulled her chair back from the table, and pushed her head down between her knees. "Breathe . . ."

She gulped air and sat up. "Jeez, girl! Your eyes started to roll back there. I'm a medic. Was a medic. Am a medic. You okay? Take a drink of your coffee. Didn't mean to scare you. I don't know where our mom is. Or our dad for that matter. Last I heard she was in Oklahoma, shacked up with some oil-rich Indian, drinking themselves to death. But I don't know what's true, what's not true, about that one. You gonna live?"

Cash drank coffee. Nodded. He was sitting across the table from her again. Lighting another cigarette. Offering her one. She took it. Even though it was Camel straight. She took a big drag and felt the smoke burn her lungs. Bits of tobacco sat on her tongue. She picked them off with her fingertips. She eyed his name tag on his army shirt. LT. SIVERTSON.

"Yeah. Sivertson. Not Blackbear," he said through a haze of smoke. "Might change my name back now that I've been disinherited. When they adopted me, they changed my first name from Fred to Paul. Needed a "Christian" name. Shit don't matter. Folks now just call me Geronimo. Mo for short. Folks think I joke like Mo on the Three Stooges. Then they get to know me. Ger-ro-ni-MO!" He laughed. "I came by after closing time but you weren't here."

"I drive beet truck."

"Parked my car in some park down by the river. Woke up with a cramp in my leg and needed to piss. Came back by here and decided to see if you were home."

"I go to school. I gotta get ready to go to school." Cash drank the last of her coffee, standing up.

"Mind if I crash here?"

Cash looked around her small apartment, which was only a kitchenette, bath and a living room she used as a bedroom.

Mo was watching her look around. "Look, I'll just throw my stuff on the floor against the wall over here in the kitchen. Drier than a rice paddy and way fewer mosquitos. Not used to this cold anymore. Sleeping inside will be good."

"Sure." Cash went into the bedroom and grabbed

some clean jeans and a T-shirt off the easy chair she used as a closet. From the dresser drawer she got undies and socks. She went into the bathroom and closed the door. When it didn't quite shut, the wood swollen from years of summer humidity, she realized she had probably never shut it before. She pushed it a bit until it stuck although there was still a crack of light. She dressed quickly, brushed her teeth and hair and finally looked at herself in the mirror.

Why'd you almost pass out? She stood staring at herself, scared brown eyes welled with tears staring back. *Fuck that.* She splashed her face with cold water. She grabbed her bath towel and scrubbed her face dry. *Get your ass to school.*

When she came out of the bathroom, Mo was stretched out on the floor against the north wall. His mattress was an army blanket and his rucksack was his pillow. He barely opened his eyes. "Just checking my eyelids for holes," he said before closing them again.

Cash grabbed her books off the table and ran down the wooden stairs. The cool autumn air filled her lungs and she got a bit light-headed again. *Knock it off.* She jumped in the Ranchero, drove a block down the street and parked face in at the Casbah. Shorty saw her coming and gave her a stern look. "Don't start," she told him. "Just give me a Bud. I'm going to test out of my English and maybe my science class. I don't have to be there right now."

Shorty pushed a Bud across the bar. "You can't make this a habit. I'll quit serving you."

Cash laughed. She took a big gulp. "Where's Ol' Man Willie?"

"You beat him in this morning, girl. You can't be doing this."

"Two mornings . . . two mornings out of my whole damn life, not gonna turn me into Willie."

"You're just a kid, Cash—you don't have a 'whole damn life' to be talking about. Some Army guy was in here asking for you last night, by the way."

"I know. He found me."

"Your brother?"

"I guess. I gotta go to class. Pretty sure I passed the test to get out of my English class. The sooner I can get back to drinking nights, you won't have to serve me in the mornings." Cash put her money on the counter and left.

The beer had gone down on an empty stomach but at least it had settled her nerves. She drove from Fargo, across the Red River into Moorhead on the

Minnesota side of the river. She was too early for classes, especially since she was sure she passed the English test. She headed north on Highway 75, drove the speed limit. Passed through the small towns of Kragnes, Georgetown, Perley and Hendrum, each town an orange and yellow tree-filled oasis on the flat prairie that was now mostly black, plowed fields. The trees along the river were golden. They shimmered in the morning sun. When she got to what folks called the four-mile corner, four miles before the township of Halstad, she made a U-turn and headed back toward Moorhead at the same snail's pace, speedometer right on the speed limit.

She lit up a cigarette and rolled down the car window a bit so the smoke blew out behind her. She didn't know what to think. The last time she had seen him was when they were riding in the car just before their mother rolled it in the ditch.

Back then, he was a scrawny, underfed kid. His baby teeth rotted before his six-year front teeth could fall out. His crew cut was never cut soon enough, so it always looked like a rooster's head. She vaguely remembered her sister—Chi-chi, they called her. Chi-chi had been scrawny too, but her hair had been long and curly, always matted in back because it never got brushed.

Cash had long ago given up wondering where they were, how they were, why no one ever came for her. Hope itself became a burden too big to bear. With no family and left alone to endure the constant abuse of foster homes, there were nights she went to sleep hoping to not wake. Other times she almost convinced herself that dream time was real time and wake time was dream time. But then reality would hit. As young as she was, she grasped the idea that each day was as good as it was going to get. And so she gave up the hope of rescue, of family returning, of something different. With hope gone, at eleven years old, she had taken to furtively smoking cigarettes and drinking beer, both of which seemed to make it all a bit more bearable.

It wasn't until Wheaton moved her into her own apartment in Fargo, rescuing her from an abusive foster dad, that Cash became more self-determined. She finished high school and kept working farm labor. Now Wheaton had signed her up for college. While he seemed to see a future for her, Cash still doubted the world was in her favor. She lived day to day, trusting no one, spending most of her time alone. Her closest friends were her cue stick and the Ranchero. And the river that flowed to the north. And the land that gave life to wheat and corn and sugar beets. The flat plains that gave her room to breathe.

A hawk flew over the Ranchero, low enough for Cash to tell it was a red-tailed hawk. She flicked her cigarette butt out the car window and rolled it all the way down. The cool breeze helped clear her brain. She hoped she had passed the English test and hoped she passed the science one too. She needed to not be worried about some folks who hadn't been too concerned about her so far in her life. Mo needed a place to sleep away from mosquitos. She had a place for him. He was already asleep, not thinking about her at all. She needed to focus. Pass these classes. Get out of the brick classrooms.

She pulled into the Piggly Wiggly parking lot in Moorhead. The store was open with a few station wagons scattered about the parking lot—farm wives doing some shopping. Cash ran in and bought four jelly-filled Bismarck donuts wrapped in plastic. Back in the Ranchero she tore them open and bit into one. In a habit developed in childhood, she started eating the Bismarck on a rounded edge away from the jelly, saving the jelly-filled center for last. She wiped her sticky hands on her jeans and took a drink of coffee from her Thermos.

She found a parking spot near campus and walked to the Science building. Sharon was standing on the building steps, scanning the campus. When she caught sight of Cash, she came running over.

"There you are! I've been looking all over for you. I met with Mr. Danielson yesterday for my extra credit. He was the perfect gentleman. He didn't make any kind of pass at me at all. We were squished into his tiny office. I could barely breathe from being so close to him. I don't know what to do. What should I do?"

Cash raised her eyebrows.

"I'm gonna die," wailed Sharon.

Cash shook her head. "Do you go to the school football games?"

"No. Why? Everyone says he makes it with students. What's wrong with me?"

"Why don't you go to the games?"

"I don't know. They're, like, for jocks and cheerleaders. The sorority crowd. Do I look like sorority crowd? Aiiiiii—that's what's wrong. Maybe he likes the sorority type."

"Knock it off. Is there a game this weekend?"

"There is every weekend, as far as I know. Till Homecoming anyways. We haven't already had Homecoming, have we?"

Cash stopped them up short on a bulletin board inside the Science building.

"Look, Homecoming is *this* weekend. We should go."

"No, we shouldn't. Teachers and jocks. Sorority sisters and old folks. Not our crowd, Cash. Not our crowd. Besides, tomorrow night we're going to the Indian students' potluck."

"Yeah, but the game is on Saturday. Come on, I'll pay your way in? Maybe Mr. Danielson is going," Cash bribed.

"And you'll tell the dorm I'm staying with you and your 'dad'? And I won't have to sneak out to see Chaské?"

"Yep."

"GOOD MORNING, SHARON. MORNING, RENEE," Mr. Danielson greeted them as they entered his classroom. Cash immediately glanced to the back of the room to make sure her spot was empty. It was. Sharon sashayed to the empty seat in the front row. "I'd like a word with you after class, Renee," he said before turning to write more notes on the board.

Sharon turned around in her seat, eyebrows raised in question. Cash shrugged. It was a long, boring hour.

Cash doodled cattails and leafless trees as she waited for it to pass.

When the bell rang, she gathered her books. Sharon waited for her by Mr. Danielson's desk. "I understand you've asked to test out of my class."

Cash clutched her notebooks to her chest. Sharon raised her eyebrows behind Mr. Danielson's back. Cash nodded her head yes.

"Well, you've certainly had good quiz scores. You're taking the test tomorrow?"

Cash nodded yes again.

"You know I teach the next level science class, also. If you pass, I hope you'll consider taking it. Or maybe I'll see you back here Monday." He flashed her a charming smile.

Cash nodded and hugged her books tighter. She looked at Sharon before turning and leaving the classroom. Sharon followed her out.

"Why are you doing that?" Sharon whispered loudly.

"I already know most of the stuff he's teaching. If I test out of this class and English, I won't have to get up so early after working nights," Cash whispered back.

"Well, I'm staying in his class just so I can look at him."

"I'm going to the rec hall before my next class. Come on."

"No, unlike some folks, I have to study. I'll see you tomorrow. And are you going to cook something for the potluck?" Cash looked at her, dumbfounded.

"They said it was potluck. That means we're supposed to bring something for everyone to eat."

"I don't cook."

"Well, they said beer—or you could bring a package of cookies from the store."

Cash puffed her cheeks and blew out, frustrated. "I'll see."

Instead of going to the rec hall, Cash went to her Ranchero. She rolled down both windows and sat looking out at the passing students and cars while she ate another Bismarck.

She thought about the Tweed girl. About Gunner, the gunnysack dog rescued by Wheaton. She rewrote the English essay about Shakespeare and Langston Hughes in her head. When her mind circled around to the brother sleeping upstairs in her apartment, she sent it back to estimating her next pay from hauling beets. She licked her fingers and wiped them on her jeans, rolled up the truck windows and walked back over to the rec hall to shoot pool until her psych class.

After school, she didn't want to go back to her apartment. Not yet. She decided to stop at Piggly Wiggly and grab some cookies for the potluck. She stood in the cookie aisle for a good twenty minutes. There were so many choices. Which ones would the other students want to eat? Chocolate chip? Molasses? Sugar cookies? She felt sick to her stomach.

Another woman came into the aisle pushing a cart brimming with groceries. Judging by the cereal boxes, Cash had to assume she had a bunch of kids. Well-fed farm kids.

The overflowing cart pushed Cash back into a memory of sitting at a kitchen table in a foster home. All the other kids—the family's "real" kids—were eating some new sugar-coated, berry-flavored cereal while arguing over which one was going to be the first to order the kite on the back of the box. They were laughing and teasing each other. The biggest one said he would send the smallest one up on the kite first as a test case. The second biggest one had said, "No, no, send Renee, not our baby." They all laughed harder. A thin spray of milk shot from one or the other's mouth as they laughed their way through their morning meal. Cash sat hunched over her bowl of Corn Flakes, the cheap cereal, the cereal she was allowed to eat.

The mom pushing the cart interrupted Cash's memory with a soft, "Excuse me," and reached past Cash to get a package of wafer cookies. The pink, brown and vanilla ones—long, thin and crunchy.

When she was gone, Cash grabbed the same kind of wafer cookie and headed to the checkout counter with the shortest line. The woman ahead of her and the cashier were in a hushed discussion with a lot of *tsk-tsking* going on. Cash moved closer to eavesdrop.

"Gone. Just like that Tweed girl."

"How? From where?

"They don't know. Down south. Some little town, like Melon or Milan. Right on the border, I heard."

"She didn't just run away? Kids these days are hitchhiking all around the country."

"No. A high school student. Top student. She just won some award or other and was in the newspapers all over the state."

"What's this world coming to? Hippies. Anti-war protesters. We're not safe anywhere anymore."

"You take care, Hazel," the cashier said as the bag boy finished bagging the woman's groceries and the cashier started ringing up Cash's cookies.

"Just the cookies?"

"Yep," said Cash, laying her money on the counter.

Cash wished she had the nerve to chase after Hazel and ask her about the other missing girl. Instead she took her package of cookies and drove across the river to her apartment.

She sat in the Ranchero outside her place, smoking a Marlboro, blowing the smoke out the window. *Go on, girl, it's your apartment. Go on.* Leaving the cookies on the seat along with the two leftover Bismarcks, she got out of the truck and trudged up the stairs.

Even before she opened the door, she could smell marijuana. She jerked the door open to find her brother sitting at her kitchen table, a joint burning in the ashtray along with one of his filterless cigarettes. In front of him were a decent size pile of marijuana and about forty rolled joints. "Get that shit out of here," she hollered at him.

He looked up at her, amused.

"Don't get your undies in a bunch, little sis."

His talk was slow. His movements slow too, as he carefully finished rolling the joint he was working on and stacked it with the others.

"Wanna toke?" He held out the joint from the ashtray.

"You need to get that shit out of my apartment."

"Hey! Hey!" He raised his hands as if she were

holding a gun on him. He carefully put the joints into small plastic sandwich bags. The first time he lost count so he ended up counting them twice, his glazed eyes and slow movements evidence that he'd smoked a bit more than just the joint in the ashtray. Cash stood, arms crossed, glaring at him.

"Relax, little sis. Look, I'm doing what you asked," he said as he put the pile of weed into a small paper bag and carefully folded it over many times from the top.

"You need to get that shit out of my apartment," Cash repeated.

"Okay. Okay." He got up slowly and went to his duffle bag, still on the floor near the north wall, Army blanket folded neatly next to it. He rummaged around and came back with a large black plastic garbage bag. He put the joints and paper bag of weed in the larger bag.

"Back in a flash, little sis," he said, letting the screen door slam shut behind him, causing him to duck, before realizing it was the door. He saw Cash watching him and laughed at himself, gave her a small salute and headed down the stairs.

Cash sat down on a chair, then got up to heat a cup of coffee for herself. She wondered briefly about throwing Mo out of her apartment, but he seemed eager enough to please her and had taken the marijuana out of her house willingly. Once she had her cup, she poured the grounds out of the coffeepot and made a new pot. Damn, she'd forgotten to grab a sandwich from the Silver Cup. When that pot of coffee was made, she refilled her Thermos after emptying out the coffee from the day before. She wondered if her brother was coming back. She needed to leave for work. She grabbed her work clothes off the floor by her bed and went into the bathroom to change. When she came out, her brother was sitting at the kitchen table. *Goddam*n, she thought; she hadn't heard him come in at all.

"It's cool, little sis, it's cool. I forgot you're friends with the fuzz. Won't happen again."

"I gotta go to work." Cash stood in her small kitchen.

"Okay if I crash here for a bit? Just in that corner. No more smoke. Promise. Maybe I'll go down to your bar tonight and shoot a few games."

"I guess." Halfway down the stairs, she turned around and went back up and into her bedroom. She opened her dresser and took out the roll of money she kept stashed there in the bottom of a drawer. *Just in case.* She stuck it in her jacket pocket and walked out again. "Later," she said on her way out. He was at the kitchen table, shuffling a deck of cards.

She stuffed the money up into the springs of the car seat. He might be her brother, but she didn't know him from Adam. Just after she put the truck into gear, the passenger door opened. The truck jerked forward and stalled out. "What the hell?" she hollered.

Her brother was leaning in the passenger door, grinning.

"Wanna go eat? You must have to eat before you go to work."

He was already sitting inside, picking up the cookies she had bought. He looked like he was ready to rip them open. Cash grabbed them out of his hands and stuffed them under her seat.

"Those are for a meeting tomorrow night."

"Come on. Let's go eat. I'll buy. Starvin' Marvin. That's me. Starvin' Marvin. Don't you cook? Ain't nothing in that fridge. No wonder you're so tiny—you don't eat."

He was grinning at her. What bothered Cash is the grin didn't quite get to his eyes. He didn't seem mean, but wary or cautious. On edge. Maybe that was the word. On edge. Like he was constantly on the lookout for something.

"You didn't put that weed in my truck, did you?" she asked.

"Nah, man, nah. I wouldn't do that to you. Come on, let's go eat."

Cash drove to the Silver Cup. They both had the daily special, a roast beef sandwich and mashed potatoes smothered in thick gravy. They ate without talking. Shirley stared at them as she moved back and forth, but she didn't ask any questions. When they were done, Mo threw a handful of bills on the table and waved at Shirley as they walked out the door.

"I woulda sold my soul for a meal like that back in the boonies," he said, climbing into the Ranchero. "Drop me off at that bar and I'll shoot a few games. Get my exercise walking around the table. Gotta keep my girlish figure." He patted his non-existent stomach.

Cash didn't suggest that he get his exercise walking back to the bar, even though she thought about it. On the way out of Moorhead, she stopped at the liquor store and bought a twelve-pack. Driving the speed limit and watching for any cop cars, especially Wheaton— she didn't need to see Wheaton right now—she drank a beer. Once on the job, she avoided talking to any of the other drivers all night. Rather than think about her brother, or the rest of her disappeared family, she put her mind on the Tweed girl and the story she heard in Piggly Wiggly. Was it possible two girls from this farm country just decided to up and disappear?

Back when the Bakkas girl had run off with the carnie from the county fair, there were rumors of abuse in the home. People whispered about the mom whipping her for not doing the ironing fast enough. About her uncle touching her. Folks said, "She was always a wild one." Cash didn't know what was true or not, but there was a big difference between your family knowing you ran off with someone and your family not knowing where you were at all.

Where was that town they were talking about in the store? She'd never heard of a town called Melon. Miland? All she really knew was this end of the Valley, which ran from Fargo to the Canadian border. She had been in every little town along the way—and the big ones too. She'd also been in most of the towns on the North Dakota side. The farmers bought and worked land on either side of the state line. Folks talked about this side of the river or that side of the river. Rarely was the state mentioned. From what she could tell, it didn't matter to them where they farmed, as long as the topsoil was thick and produced the wheat, potatoes and beets they needed. She rummaged around in the beet truck's glove box, hoping there was a state map in there. No luck. She had one in the Ranchero.

She usually studied while she waited in line to dump a load of beets. Tonight, she threw her head back on the cracked leather seat and tried to still her mind and body enough to call either girl to her. She stared up into the night sky, breathed in the crisp night air and drifted. She felt her being leave her body and float up into the air. Willing herself north, she hovered over the Tweed house in Shelly. An open circle of light invited her down into the girl's bedroom, where once again the sweater hung. This time it glittered like the stars overhead, though there was nothing new there to see or feel. Cash's being zoomed up and out of the same circle of light and willed herself to go south. She floated along the river, skimming the treetops. She felt neither cold nor wind, just a gentle floating, like lying in an inner tube floating on a still lake.

She passed over Fargo–Moorhead, the city lights below mirroring the flickering stars above. She followed the Red as far south as it went. She didn't dare leave her familiar landmark, the river she had known all her life. A series of truck horns jerked her back into her body. It was like the rubber on a slingshot had been released. She started the truck rapidly, shifted the gears and moved forward in line.

One of the other beet-haulers popped up in her driver's window when she came to a stop, tapping on the glass. His unshaven face, half-covered by a farmer's hat, peered in at her. She rolled down her window.

"You fall asleep in there, Cash? You all right?"

"Yeah, I'm all right. Must have dozed off for a minute."

"Here, I got you some coffee from the shack. Nice and hot." He held up a steaming brew in a foam cup. "Another week or so and this campaign will be done. You driving this weekend? Heard some of the farmers are paying time-and-a-half, get this year done with."

"I don't know. I'll have to see."

"No one wants to be out here when the snow falls. Stay awake now."

Cash lifted the coffee cup in a salute as he hopped off the truck's running board and moved back to his own truck. She finished out her shift and returned the truck to the farmyard. She scribbled a note to Milt that she wouldn't be able to work the weekend but would be back on Monday night. She left the note on the truck dash. Once in her Ranchero, she took a drink of the Budweiser she had left open on the floorboards, lit up a Marlboro and listened to the silence of the night. Then she drove back to Fargo where she sat outside in her truck, drinking another Bud. It was past closing time and she could see the lights on in her apartment and the outline of her brother sitting at her kitchen table. She ate one of the Bismarcks that was starting to get hard, but still sweet. Washed it down with more beer.

Tomorrow, Friday, was when she was scheduled to test out of science and then there was the Indian students' meeting she had agreed to go to, had bought cookies for. And there was still most of the twelve-pack she had bought before her shift tonight. She killed the beer, grabbed another one and headed upstairs.

Mo was sitting at the table, seven empty bottles of Schlitz sitting beside him. The only indication that he might be a little drunk was his eyes were narrow slits. He grinned when she came in. He pulled a wad of ones from the pocket of his flak jacket and carelessly laid them on the table. "Here, some money for letting me stay. These jokers don't know how to shoot for shit." He laughed and dealt another card on his solitaire layout. "Got some more beer and hamburger. It's in the fridge, if you're thirsty. And eggs. Bread. Some Amerrrican food."

"I got school in the morning. Gotta sleep." Cash walked into the room where her bed was and set the beer on the dresser along with her pack of Marlboros and a matchbook. She grabbed a pair of jeans and T-shirt from her dirty pile of laundry on the floor in the corner, shook them out and sniffed them to see if they smelled like beet field. They didn't. She went into the bathroom and closed the door as best she could before peeing and pulling off the clothes she had just worked in, then put on the ones she had pulled from the laundry pile.

Back in her room she drank from the open Bud and lit up a Marlboro, staring at her brother who seemed engrossed in his solitaire game. When the beer was finished, she fluffed her pillow and lay on her side facing the window. Damn she was tired, but wired too. Not sure what to think or feel. She heard the soft *tap* of cards being laid down. She yawned. Heard the shuffle of the deck, a bottle being set down on the table. Another yawn. She put her arm over her eyes to shut out the light.

As a kid in foster homes, she had a nightly dilemma. Night wasn't always the safest time. Should she sleep with the lights off so she was harder to find in the dark? Or should she sleep with the lights on so she could see who was coming to get her? Some families forced her to shut the lights off to save electricity. Before she got older and learned better, that would send her into a tailspin of wondering, late into the night, where and how electricity was saved. You can't see electricity. Except for lightning. So just where and how was it saved? She imagined giant metal storage bins somewhere in the country filled with shooting lightning bolts.

In one home she also practiced shallow, soundless breathing, hoping to make her body harder to find. Wrapping the sheets around her, mummified, so when hands came creeping in the dark, the slightest tug would wake her and she'd sit up quickly, shoving the hands away. The hands would scurry off with the rest of the body, bare feet swishing on the hardwood floors. She yawned again and folded her pillow in half around the back of her head to shut out the sound of the cards.

CASH WOKE TO THE SMELL of bacon and the sound of grease spattering. She rolled over, pulled the pillow off her head and glanced at her alarm clock. Seven-thirty. She had a moment of panic thinking she was going to be late for English but then remembered she had taken the test to get herself out of that class. She hadn't heard yet whether she passed or not. Maybe she would run by Professor LeRoy's office first thing on campus. Her legs felt stiff and cruddy from sleeping in her jeans. The metal button on the waistband had left a red mark. She sat on the edge of her bed, stretching her legs out in front of herself. She lit up a cigarette and leaned back across the bed to open the window a couple of inches. A cool morning breeze drifted in. No frost out there that she could see. She shut the window.

She grabbed some clothes and went into the bathroom to change. Her hair was a mess. She brushed it out and wound it in a knot on top of her head with a pencil stuck through to keep it up. When she came out, there was a plate of scrambled eggs, bacon and sliced white bread sitting on the table. A steaming cup of coffee too.

"Couldn't find a toaster. Hope scrambled's okay."

Cash sat down. "Thanks," she mumbled.

He was scarfing down a plate filled with twice as much food as was on hers. "One thing I missed about being in the real world was real food. You got school, huh?"

"Yeah."

"Work?"

"No. Taking the weekend off. Got some other things I gotta do."

"They said last night there's some kinda pool tournament coming up in a couple weeks. They said you usually play, some white guy partner."

"Can't."

"Can't?"

"Got 86'd last time. Some stupid waitress accused me of stealing some beer. Sticking it in my purse."

"Did you?"

Cash breathed a heavy sigh. "I had two beers in the waistband of my pants. Under my jacket. I don't carry a stupid purse."

Mo started laughing. "So you stole the beers and they 86'd you for stealing."

"No, they 86'd me for busting up some beer bottles on my way out."

Cash by then was laughing along with him. She pantomimed clearing the table with her arm.

"What'd you do with the beer?"

"Drank it down by the river." She laughed.

"Guess we won't be playing partners at the tournament then, huh?"

"Guess not." She folded some of her scrambled egg inside one of the slices of bread and took a bite.

"So you go to school and do farm labor. Folks say you're a pretty good shot at the tables. What else you do? Got a boyfriend?"

"That's all I do. School and work."

"Boyfriend?"

"Not really."

Silence.

"You? What'd you do?"

"Just back in the world. Thought I'd be coming back to farm. No farm to farm now. Might re-up. See how the next couple weeks go. It's so quiet here. Makes me nervous. Anything exciting ever happen around here?"

"Not much. There's a girl missing from up around Shelly. And I heard yesterday another one, younger, is missing from some small town south of here."

"Missing?"

"Yeah, the one from Shelly was in my science class at school. Last week she went missing. Told her folks she was going to the Cities and never came back. Not a wild kid. Smart."

"What about the other one?"

"I don't know. Just overheard about her in the store yesterday. Some high school student. I was going to go to the library today and look back in the newspapers and see what I could find. But first I'll have to find the right town. I couldn't understand if the women were saying Melon or Myland or Midland, but they said just south of here on the border." She jumped up. "I got a map in my truck."

When she came back up, breathless from running up and down the stairs, Mo had cleared the table. She spread the map out and they leaned over it. Cash's finger traced the Red River south of Fargo–Moorhead along the Minnesota–North Dakota border. No towns that started with M. Mo was reading out loud the city and town names listed on the corner of the map. "Medina, Melrose, Mendota. Those are all too far east. Milaca. Milan. Millerville. Melville."

"Wait. Wait. Wait. Where is Milan? And Millerville?"

"Looks like Milan is on the west side of the state and Millerville way over on the east. Right here. Look, here's Milan. Right on the South Dakota border. You think that's it?"

"I don't know. I'll look it up in the newspapers when I get to school. Why would a little girl from there go missing?"

"You said she's a teenager."

"That's what the women in the store said. Said *a kid*."

"White slave trade."

"Huh?"

"White slave trade."

"What are you talking about?"

"Maybe they were kidnapped for the white slave trade." He sipped his coffee.

"Get real. You read too many true crime magazines out there in the jungle."

"No, I'm serious as a motherfucker. Boo-coo girls sold in the sex trade over in 'Nam. Round eyes carry a bigger price. Anywhere in the world for that matter, white girls—blond and blue-eyed—catch a much bigger price than anyone else."

"No-o."

"It happens. That's what I'd be looking for if I had two girls disappear like that." He drank some more coffee. "Girls that ain't ever been in trouble? Sure as shit, they been kidnapped."

Cash finished her lukewarm coffee. "That's sick. I gotta get to school."

She put the coffee cup in the sink, then filled her Thermos with the rest of the coffee from the coffeepot. She grabbed her cigarettes and matches off the table and left.

She shivered as she waited for the heat in the

Ranchero to kick in. She didn't believe her brother. She had been through some crap in her life, but even with that, she couldn't imagine what he was saying.

As soon as she got to school, she stopped by the English department. She knocked on the professor's door but there was no answer. There was an envelope taped to the doorframe with the name "Renee Black-bear" written on it. She opened the envelope. On a half-sheet of paper was written, *You passed. I'd like to talk to you about your essay.*

Leroy, barely legible, was scrawled across the bottom.

Yes! she thought, stuffing the note into her back pocket.

Next she went to the campus library. The building was quiet and smelled of old paper. Dust motes drifted in the light from the windows. Cash looked around warily. She was used to the Bookmobile that would come to the farm towns every two weeks. You entered at the driver's end. The mobile van had shelves of books lining either wall. One side held children's books, the other adult books. When Cash first started going to the Bookmobile, the librarian tried to steer her to the children's side of the van. Back then Cash didn't talk to anyone, so she checked out *Island of the Blue Dolphins* and *Treasure Island,* along with four adult biographies of historical figures. This continued for a summer. The librarian checked out Cash's books and asked her questions like, "Did you like that one?"

Soon she started offering Cash other books by some of the same authors. She caught Cash's interest in Indian war chiefs. Each trip a new Indian war chief book was on the ledge next to the librarian. When Cash started to read about Eastern meditation, books on meditating began to appear also.

The campus library wasn't the Bookmobile. It was a large brick building with row upon row of books, much darker and more intimidating than even the public library downtown. Cash found the seating area where the *Fargo Forum* was hanging on long wooden dowels. The oldest paper was the Sunday edition. There were a couple of other local papers and, of course, the ones from the Cities, but none from Milan.

Cash walked to the reception desk. There were a number of librarians there. She took a deep breath, blew out air and approached the one who looked the youngest. She waited for the young woman to acknowledge her, but she just kept fiddling with some index cards. Cash coughed slightly.

"Oh. May I help you?" She looked up with feigned surprise, speaking in a stage whisper.

Cash whispered back, "Newspapers from Milan, Minnesota?"

"I'm sorry?" the woman tilted her head and flipped blond hair behind her ear. "Say that again?"

Rather than speak, Cash grabbed a blank index card from the desk and a pencil and wrote, *Newspapers from Milan, Minnesota.*

"Oh. Those will all be on microfiche. Student ID please."

Cash dug it out from her back pocket. The woman read her ID slowly.

"We don't keep local newspapers on fiche here. You'd have to go to the public library." She handed the ID card back.

Cash stuffed her card back in her pocket and fled the building. *Why didn't the little twit just say that to begin with?*

The public library had more outstate newspapers than the campus library. It only took her about ten minutes to figure out the *Chippewa County News* was the paper that covered the tiny town of Milan. Sure

enough, a little over a week ago the headlines of the
county paper gave a detailed account of a young girl,
Candy Swenson, a junior at Milan High School, who
had won a Future Homemakers of America award.
She had attended the statewide FHA conference in
Minneapolis, where she disappeared from the Curtiss
Hotel, the same evening she received the award.

Vanished into thin air is how the reporter described
it. Candy sang in the Lutheran Church choir and had
two younger brothers. The reporter seemed to hint that
farm girls often came to the Cities and got attracted
to the lights and bustle, many never returning to their
homes. *Distraught*, is how the reporter described the
family and community. They vehemently denied their
daughter would ever run away.

Cash sat back and looked out the library windows.
The chair she sat on was orange fake leather that
matched some of the leaves on the trees outside. All the
years when she had hoped to escape the foster homes,
she had never achieved a workable plan. And here
were two girls, not even a hundred miles apart, whose
families loved them, wanted them—and they seemed
to have disappeared into thin air. Both were excellent
students. And, yes, her brother was right, both were
blond and blue-eyed. Cash shivered involuntarily. One

for sure had disappeared in the Cities. The other was rumored to have gone to the Cities.

Cash had heard about the Cities but had never been there. She had seen pictures in the newspaper and heard the Grain Report each day on the radio—in the morning and then again at noon. The noon report was always followed by Paul Harvey's *News and Comment* program. His gravelly voice entertained farm families up and down the Valley.

When Cash thought about the Cities, she imagined a place like Metropolis in the Superman comic books. Steel and glass. Men who wore suits every day and women in pencil skirts, wearing blouses with bows tied at the neckline.

She had a hard time imagining anyplace beyond the Valley. It wasn't something she thought about. As life became harder and harder in the foster homes, she stopped looking ahead. Gave up making plans for the future. There were mornings when despair rode the early morning sunbeams into her bedroom window. She didn't think about her future—or the next growing season or even next week. If she woke up—and so far she always had—she kept going. Drove the next truck. Plowed the next furrow. Lifted the next bale. Took the next beating, the next berating. Drank the last beer.

Smoked another cigarette. She didn't know if places like the Cities really existed. She had given up thinking that anything might be more real than what she could actually touch or feel.

Kinda like the brother sitting in her apartment. She had long ago given up thinking that they, the rest of her family, existed. Now here he was. Flesh and blood. Maybe he wasn't there. Maybe he only existed in her imagination and was only real when she was in her apartment talking with him. Sitting at the table with him.

The breakfast had been real. But maybe he wasn't there now. Like maybe he was a wisp of smoke that appeared and disappeared, took on a physical reality only when she was standing or sitting next to him. Maybe the Cities didn't really exist but were only a part of someone's imaginations, like comic book drawings. Cash tried to think if she even knew anyone who said they had been to the Cities. No one came to mind.

Shut the hell up, Cash. You're gonna drive yourself crazy. Crazier.

She slid the front page of the newspaper off the wooden dowel, looked around to make sure no one was watching her. She folded it up into a small square and put it into the pocket of her jean jacket. She hurried out of the library with her hands in her pockets.

When she got back in the Ranchero, she grabbed the steering wheel. Just grabbed the wheel and hung on. It was solid. Real. She slapped the seat beside her. The one leftover Bismarck jumped up along with a cloud of field dust. Cash grabbed it, unwrapped it from the plastic wrap and took a big bite. Raspberry jelly squirted down either side of her mouth. "Shit," she said around a mouthful of red goo, grabbing the plastic wrap and wiping her face off as best she could. Now she was really a mess. A literal mess.

On her way back to campus she stopped at the Standard Oil gas station, went to the ladies' washroom at the side of the building and threw water on her hands and face.

She drove back across the river and into Fargo, ran up the stairs to her apartment. Her brother's duffle bag was sitting against the north wall, an unfinished solitaire game laid out on the table. His half-empty coffee cup was cold. He might not be real but his stuff was. She dug the newspaper page out of her pocket, unfolded it and threw it on the table over his cards.

By habit, she opened the fridge. Damn, he had stocked it. Bacon. Eggs. Milk. Butter. What the heck was this? She pulled out a white package. Written in black crayon was the word T-bone. She put it back. She opened the tiny metal freezer. A frozen package of hamburger. The metal ice cube trays were filled. She had never checked them before, so she didn't know if Mo had done that or not. Back in the fridge, some cheese. Catsup. The bottom shelf was filled with Schlitz beer. She opened her cupboard where she kept her lone salt and pepper shakers. Elbow macaroni. Long spaghetti. Some cans of stewed tomatoes and tomato paste. Red kidney beans? Canned corn and string beans. The whole damn grocery store was in there.

The phone rang. Cash jumped, felt as if she'd been caught stealing or looking into someone else's closets. It rang again. She stood with her back to the counter. The only one who ever called her was Wheaton and she just wasn't ready to talk to him yet. She had no idea how she was going to tell him about Mo. She should tell him about the girl missing from Milan, but not now.

Instead she went into the bathroom and ran herself a bath. She grabbed clean clothes from her room while the tub filled with steaming hot water. She brought a chair in from the kitchen and propped it under the door handle. She stripped and dropped into the tub. Steam rose all around her. She redid the pencil in the knot of hair on top of her head, closed her eyes and drifted off into nowhere. Not asleep. Not awake. Not leaving her body. Just floating.

When the water grew tepid, she grabbed a washcloth and soap, lathered and rinsed herself off. The plug was on a metal chain that she pulled before she got out of the tub. The water gurgled going down as she dried off and got dressed. Clean jeans. T-shirt. Undies. Socks. She moved the chair and put it back by the kitchen table before she washed her hair in the kitchen sink. She noticed Mo had done the breakfast dishes. She looked under the sink. He'd even bought more dish soap.

Now that she was clean, she felt more settled. More together. Less scattered.

It took hours for her hair to dry, so she brushed it as best she could and twisted it into a knot on top of her head with the yellow pencil stuck through to hold it up.

Before she started out for school, she checked to make sure the wad of money was still under the seat of the Ranchero. It was. She checked behind the driver's seat and her .22 was still there too, along with her cue stick. Eight bottles of Budweiser still in the twelve-pack from the other night and a full pack of Marlboros in her jean jacket pocket. *All's right with the world.*

She got to psych class just as the students were leaving. Breathing in courage, she walked in and apologized to the professor for being late and asked if there was an assignment for the weekend. She gave Cash the day's handout without question and said, "See you next week."

From psych, Cash went to the science building. The dean's door was open. Without looking up from the papers he was grading, he gestured for her to come in. She stood right inside the door until he stood up, grabbed the papers he had been working on and another thin booklet and said, "Follow me."

Forty-five minutes later, Cash was exiting the science building. She felt confident that she had passed. The whole test seemed as easy as a ninth-grade multiple-choice final exam. Cash felt light. Things were going along as planned. *Casbah, here I come.* Once beet season was over, one more week, two at the most, she would be home free. She started across campus to judo class.

"Renee. Renee Blackbear."

It took a few seconds for it to register that someone was calling her name. Another adjustment in college.

Folks called her by her legal name. She looked up as Professor LeRoy came scuttling across campus toward her. He was a little heavyset and his pants were belted below his waist. His starched shirt stretched across his rounded belly. He had some papers in his hand, waving them in the air.

"Did you get my note?"

"Yes."

He caught up with her. "I need to talk with you about your essay. It was excellent! It was such short notice, I didn't have time to get ahold of you. I did call your home once. No one answered. I tried again this morning."

"Oh."

"You wouldn't have seen it—mostly the upper-grads applied—there was a statewide competition for essays by minority students. I couldn't reach you, but I knew your essay was a contender, a real contender, so I, um, submitted it for you. As your professor. And by golly if it didn't get accepted as one of the finalists for the state. They are deciding the winner next weekend down in the Cities, at Macalester College. Big honor. You gotta go."

Cash shifted her weight from one foot to the other. "Huh?"

LeRoy slowed down. "The essay you wrote to test out of English 101? One of the best I've ever seen. I submitted it to the statewide competition. I got word this morning your essay is a contender. I already checked out a state vehicle. The award ceremony is next weekend at Macalester College in St. Paul, down in the Cities. I'll drive us down. Great honor for you. Great honor for our English department. Such a stroke of genius to decide to test out of 101."

Cash took the piece of paper he was waving around in his hands. It was addressed to her, c/o Professor LeRoy, Moorhead State English Department. It said just what he was saying: Her essay was a contender for the state prize. Award Ceremony, Saturday, October 11th. Seven P.M. Cash looked at him. He was grinning. Pleased, almost as if he single-handedly had taught her everything she knew.

"You'll go, right? I already checked out a state vehicle. I'll drive us down. Macalester has a Minority Students' House they'll let you stay at overnight."

Her stomach clenched. Cash did not ride anywhere with anyone, other than the occasional ride with Wheaton. And since getting her own apartment, she'd never slept in another bed except her own. She wasn't about to start now.

She read the letter again. Never in her life had she imagined anything like this. She looked at Professor LeRoy. The excitement in his eyes and his silly grin made her smile.

"I got a car," she said. "I could follow you down."

He took the letter from her hand. He seemed perplexed. But he brightened quickly. "Sure. We can do that. It's about a four-hour drive. If we met here at ten next Saturday morning, we'd be there early afternoon. Plenty of time to sightsee and find the minority house."

Cash didn't tell him she had no intention of sleeping in the minority house, whatever that was, but she would deal with that issue later.

"Let's meet at the school carpool. You know where that is? Over by the field house."

"Yep."

"Ten A.M. Sharp!" He waved the paper in his hand.

"Sure," said Cash.

He spun and walked away bouncing on his toes.

Cash didn't know what to think. The Cities. Guess she would find out if they were real. Like everything else in her life, a possible award was another blank molecule, an unknown in the universe, not another thing to hope for or not hope for. Just something to tuck away in the deeper recesses of her mind and see what might happen, if anything.

After judo she took a quick shower in the girls' locker room, keeping her head and hair out from under the water spray. If she didn't get it wet, her hair might be dry enough to brush through by the time of the potluck tonight. She looked at the clock on the gym wall. Four-thirty. Plenty of time for a few practice shots on the tables in the rec hall.

At 6:30, she couldn't avoid it any longer. She'd bought the cookies, she had committed to going to the potluck, now she had to go. She brushed her hair out with her fingers, then pulled a hairbrush out of her glove box. She managed to get it into a loose braid before driving to Mrs. Kills Horses' house.

Cash was so nervous she didn't dare drink a beer on the way even though she knew that would have calmed her nerves. She sat in the Ranchero, watching the Kills Horses' house. The sun was going down, but the curtains were still open. The lights were on, and she could see people by the front window. Mrs. Kills Horses was talking rapidly with her hands and arms.

A tap on the car window made her jump. She looked over to see a longhaired Indian dude grinning at her through the glass. As she rolled down the window, the smell of Patchouli almost knocked her out.

"You must be Cash. Sharon told me you drove a Ranchero. Sweet ride." He leaned back on his heels and whistled softly, stretching his arms out the length of the truck. "Sharon's gonna be late. Said she had an important meeting with her science teacher. Discuss her grades or somethin'. I don't know what she's worried about. She always gets A's. You goin' in or you just gonna window peep?"

Cash reached over and grabbed the cookies and beer off the car seat. "I was just getting ready to go in."

"Here, let me grab the beer."

Cash would have felt silly with just the cookies in her hand so she shook her head no and held on to the beer. The guy was carrying a paper bag. He held it up.

"Sharon came by early this morning and made tuna hot dish in our dorm kitchen."

"She's talking to the science teacher?"

"Yeah. You know these people here?"

"No. Just the counselor, Mrs. Kills Horses."

"Sharon said she thought you were gonna get jumped in the rec hall."

"Nah."

Just then, Mrs. Kills Horses opened her front door.

"Come in. Come in," she gushed. She was wearing skintight blue jeans, a white blouse opened to show lots of cleavage. She had pounds of turquoise and silver jewelry on her neck, her arms and fingers, displayed as if her blood quantum were equal to silver grams. She was wearing the new platform heels all the hippie chicks were wearing. "You can put the beer in the fridge. Help yourself to food on the table. Let me take that from you." She took the paper bag from Sharon's boyfriend, saying, "I haven't seen you around school."

"I go to NDSU. From the Aberdeen area."

"Well, welcome. Good for everyone to meet everyone. And your name?"

"Chaské."

"Kids! Everyone. This is Chaské. He goes to NDSU. And some of you know Renee?"

"Cash."

"Yes, Renee likes to go by Cash. You met Tezhi. His girlfriend, Bunk. She's another one who prefers to use her nickname. What did you say your real name is Bunk?" When Bunk ignored the question, Mrs. Kills Horses rushed to fill the silence by saying, "And this is her cousin, Marlene." She rattled off the other six or eight students' names so quickly Cash didn't catch them. She could see the fridge in the kitchen from where she was standing, so she made a beeline to it and put the beer in, coming back with one in her hand even though it was kinda warm from sitting in the car all day and night. The couch was full of students. Chaské had taken a pillow on the floor. Cash sat down on a pillow beside him.

"Come on. Come on. Eat." Mrs. Kills Horses put a roaster of sloppy joe meat on the table beside hamburger buns. "Lots for everyone."

The other students lined up and filled their plates. Chaské and Cash pulled themselves up off the pillows to be last in line. The table was filled with food. As Cash dished up, it occurred to her that she'd eaten more in the last twenty-four hours than she'd eaten in the whole past month.

But the food was good. She watched the other students go back for seconds. It was easy to tell which kids had come from homes where there hadn't been much. They ate fast. And a lot. Sharon's tuna casserole reminded Cash of Lutheran Ladies' Aid meetings. The sloppy joe sandwiches of high school football games. No one used the paper napkins Mrs. Kills Horses had put out on the table, they just wiped their hands on their jeans. By the time Cash went through the line, she only got one of her pink cookies. And there had been a rush for her beer as soon as she walked away from the fridge. It looked like most of the students had kept their six-packs on the floor by their feet. *Lesson learned.*

Barely anyone talked while they ate except Mrs. Kills Horses. She talked enough for everyone, filling any quiet space with useless chatter. After everyone quit going back for seconds and thirds, Mrs. Kills Horses decided it was time to elect officials for the Indian Students' Association. She cheerily called for volunteers for president, vice president and secretary-treasurer. No one acknowledged her enthusiastic request. Cash saw Tezhi elbow his girlfriend, Bunk, who in turn elbowed her cousin, Marlene. Marlene then elbowed Bunk, who elbowed Tezhi.

The movement caught Mrs. Kills Horses' eye. "Tezhi? Are you volunteering to run for president?"

Bunk lifted his arm. "Right on," she answered for him.

Marlene, barely above a whisper said, "And Bunk for vice president."

"And what about you for secretary-treasurer?" Mrs. Kills Horses asked Marlene in a sweet voice.

Marlene dropped her head.

"Okay! Anyone else want to run for one of these positions?" Mrs. Kills Horses asked the group.

Everyone dropped their heads, looked at their plates or shook their head back and forth.

"Okay! Well, we still need to vote. Can we just do it by show of hands?" Without waiting for an answer, she asked, "All those in favor of Tezhi being president of the Indian Students' Association?"

All hands went up.

The process was repeated for vice president and secretary-treasurer with no dissenting votes.

Mrs. Kills Horses clapped her hands. She was the only one to do so. "Congratulations to our new student officers. Tezhi, do you want to take over from here as new president?"

"Uh, what do I do?" he asked.

"Because it's a new school year and this is the first time we've had an Indian Students' Association here at Moorhead State, we really don't have any old business, so I guess you could just open it up for any new business."

"Any new business?" Tezhi asked.

Bunk answered, "Remember we were talking about seeing if we could get AIM to come up here. Talk to the student body. Maybe help us figure out how to have control over our financial aid money."

Students started nodding.

"How do we get ahold of them?" someone asked.

Bunk answered, "Marlene's aunt lives in the Cities. She said she would talk to them for us."

Someone else asked, "When are we talking about? I hate having to make a list for the registrar for every little thing I need."

"I can pay for my own books. I don't know why I gotta go to them every time I need a pencil or some macaroni to cook."

"I know, that lady in the registrar's office gets all nosy, asking why I need money for this or that. It's my money. I'm sick of telling her my life story every time I need some cash. It's our money."

"Yeah, yeah," echoed around the room.

"How we gonna pay for AIM?" another one asked.

"Minority affairs have given us a small budget for cultural activities. I think if we planned a late fall powwow and invited AIM up as guest speakers for our cultural event, we could get the whole thing covered," Mrs. Kills Horses chimed in.

Cash was getting bored. *Where the hell was Sharon?* she wondered. All her beer in the fridge was gone, cigarette smoke was drifting around the room, her stomach was full and it was getting pretty stuffy. She looked at Chaské. He was sitting cross-legged, elbows on knees, hands on chin, looking engrossed in the conversation, but when she shifted off the pillow and stood up, he hopped up too, whispering, "Ready to book?"

Yes.

"Me, too. Let's boogie."

He walked over to the table and retrieved Sharon's empty tuna casserole bowl. Mrs. Kills Horses followed them to the front door, hoped they had a good time, wished them a good evening, hoped to see them next week at school and at the next meeting, and thanked them for coming while Cash and Chaské slipped out, bombarded by her well-meaning-ness.

As soon as they were on the sidewalk, Cash said, "Where is Sharon? She said she'd be here."

Chaské didn't seem too worried or upset at all. He shrugged. "You know how she is. Catch a ride back to Fargo?"

"Sure."

Chaské got out at her apartment on NP Avenue and said he'd walk or hitchhike back to NDSU. If Sharon wasn't already there, she'd show up soon, he was sure. Cash caught a whiff of weed as he lit up walking away from her.

Upstairs in her apartment, a game of solitaire was laid out on the table, the duffle still in the corner. No brother in sight, but the dishes in the sink were done and a dark blue sheet nailed across the archway that separated her bedroom from the kitchen area. Cash opened the fridge. No Bud but there was a Schlitz. Better than nothing, she guessed. She popped the top and sat down at the kitchen table in "her" spot that had now become her brother's spot somehow. She played the solitaire game, flipping and moving cards slowly, drank the beer and smoked a couple of cigarettes.

Mo was probably at one of the bars on the avenue. She didn't have to work. It wasn't even 8:30. She could go to the Casbah if she wanted. She could drive up toward Ada and try to catch Wheaton. Tell him about the other girl who was missing. Yeah, that's probably what she should do. Once she talked with him, there'd still be time to shoot a few games.

She flipped another card over—the ten of hearts didn't have a place anywhere on the layout. She scooped up all the cards, shuffled them a few times and laid out a new game, ready for Mo whenever he returned.

She threw the beer bottle in the trash and headed out, taking Highway 75 north toward Halstad on the off chance that Wheaton might be patrolling on this

Friday night. No luck. She turned at the four-mile corner and headed east to Ada. He wasn't on that road either. When she got into Ada, she could see that the field lights were on over by the high school. She headed that way.

The bleachers were filled with students dressed in wool coats, scarves around their necks against the fall chill. She could hear the cheerleaders chanting as she pulled up. Older farm couples sat in the cars parked head-on toward the field. Some had the engines running, heaters turned up against the night air. Others had windows cracked, cigarette smoke drifting out. The air smelled of dry leaves, popcorn and hotdogs. Cash found a spot to park. She pulled the Ranchero in line with the other head-on cars. She got out and walked the length of Ada's side of the field. She found Wheaton's cruiser at the far end but he wasn't in it, so she walked back up toward the bleachers and peered up and down at the folks seated there before she saw him standing, leaning against the wooden railing that served as a fence a bit farther down.

The student body in the bleachers erupted in a wild screaming cheer as the Ada Tigers offense lined up in an attempt at a touchdown. Cash looked at the scoreboard. The Tigers were in a narrow lead. The cheerleaders amped up their routine. "T-O-U-C-H-D-O-W-N. Touch-down!"

The quarterback handed the ball to the tight end who ran it into the end zone. The hometown crowd surged forward. Folks jumped out of cars and rushed as close to the sidelines as they could get. The crowd seemed to double in size. Cash had to push her way to where Wheaton was standing.

He was wearing a wool jacket, the sheriff's emblem on the jacket's left shoulder. It was a similar cut and style to all the high school letterman jackets in the county. Except his was a plain brown, almost an Army brown, and the students sported their high school colors: Ada's being orange and black, the opposing team red and white.

Wheaton had his hands cupped around his mouth, hollering, "Way to go, Harry Jr. Way to go." In the cold night air, steam surrounded his words. Cash came and stood beside him. Harry Jr. turned circles in the end zone, the football held high over his head as his teammates came around him and slapped his back. The ref's whistle blew and the teams lined up for the extra point.

Wheaton looked down when he felt Cash stand next to him. "Hey, kid, what are you doing here?"

"Yeah, football really ain't my thing, you know. But, hey, go Tigers."

Cash pumped her fist. They both laughed.

"Game's almost over. Looks like the home team is gonna win."

They stood and watched the remainder of the game. Cash had to stamp her feet, jump up and down a few times to keep warm. She wished she had worn a sweatshirt under her jean jacket.

Then the game was over, the crowd cheering and hooting. Car lights flashed off and on as horns honked. The Tigers lined up and shook hands with the opposing team. The cheerleaders, in their short, pleated skirts and orange and white wool sweaters, chanted, "V-I-C-T-O-R-Y, that's the Tiger's victory cry," while doing high kicks.

As Wheaton and Cash walked through the crowd, men clapped his shoulder as if he were a member of the winning team. Cash wondered if any of them were his friend or if the jovial behavior was an attempt to garner favor for future speeding tickets or late-night disturbances in one of the local bars. Each time someone touched him or said, "Good evening, Sheriff," Wheaton raised his hand in a wave, responded with, "Same to you," all the while continuing a steady pace to his cruiser.

"I parked over there," said Cash. "Where should I meet you?"

"We could drive over to Twin Valley. That restaurant stays open a bit later. Everything here closes down at sunset."

"Okay, I'll follow you."

Cars were backing up and forming a line to exit the field. Wheaton moved off to the side, engine idling, waiting for her. She pulled up behind his car, followed him all the way to the small town of Twin Valley, fourteen miles to the east of Ada.

The café was still open, empty except for the waitress sipping coffee at the counter and reading the newspaper. She walked over with two white coffee cups and a half-full glass carafe. The coffee smelled like it had been brewing a few hours. She set the cups down and filled them. "We still have some blueberry pie left. Or did you want burgers?"

Wheaton looked at Cash, eyebrows raised.

"Pie is good."

"I'll take the same," said Wheaton.

The waitress walked across the linoleum floor, a black and white checkerboard square pattern, marred by chair scrapings and work shoes. When she was behind the counter getting the pies from the glass carousel, Wheaton asked, "So, what brought you to Ada?"

Cash sipped her coffee. "Did you know there is another girl missing?"

"From school?" His coffee cup stopped midway to his mouth.

"No, a little town south of Fargo–Moorhead. Milan. I'm not sure how to pronounce it exactly. It's spelled M-i-l-a-n."

"Where'd you learn this?"

"I was at Piggly Wiggly and overheard a couple women talking. They said this girl was missing from some small town south of us. I went to the Moorhead Library and checked it out in the newspapers."

The waitress arrived back at the table with two plates of blueberry pie. The crust was light brown with a thin sprinkling of sugar on it. Cash touched her fork to the sugar and then licked it, savoring the sweetness.

Wheaton was half done while she was still chewing her first bite.

"So, what did you find out in the papers?"

"That she's a junior in high school. She won an FHA award and went down to the Cities to receive the award. Disappeared from the Curtiss Hotel. Been almost two weeks missing." Cash finished her pie and scraped the crust and remaining sugar off the plate and into her mouth.

"That's it?"

"Yeah, she's a good student. Blond, blue-eyed, looks like all the girls around here. Her family says she'd never run away."

Wheaton looked into the distance, over Cash's shoulder, out the restaurant window. "That's it?"

"That's it."

Both of them sipped coffee. The waitress returned to refill their cups and remove the pie plates.

"Where's Gunner?"

"At home. I didn't want to leave him in the cruiser while I was at the game. Hope he doesn't tear up my other shoes. Last time I left him alone, he ate my slippers."

"What's the white slave market?"

"White slave market? Where'd you hear that?"

"Some guy," lied Cash. She wasn't ready to tell Wheaton about the brother crashing in her apartment. "Some guy was saying that maybe the Tweed girl got kidnapped into the white slave market. He said white girls can be sold for a lot on that market."

"I suppose there is some truth to that."

"But what is it?"

"Folks, men, selling women into prostitution. There have been rumors that sometimes girls from up around here don't run away, they're taken. Introduced to life on the streets. Given drugs. And then turned into prostitutes."

"Prostitutes? They sell themselves for sex?" Cash was having a hard time understanding the conversation. When she was in school, there were girls who were called whores. Everyone knew they slept with boys. In the small towns in the Valley, there were codes of what was okay and what was not. If the captain of the football team and the captain of the cheerleading squad were going steady, after a few years it was assumed they had "gone all the way" because, of course, they were going to get married right after high school. If a girl "went all the way" with one or more boys and wasn't going steady, the word whore was whispered around the school halls.

Even making out with too many boys could get a girl labeled a whore. Or being the Indian foster girl in a new school, even if you didn't make out with anyone. What Cash knew about prostitutes was what she had read in books or seen on TV westerns. Women in saloons, for one. It was hinted in the storyline that they would have sex for money.

This didn't seem to be what Wheaton or Mo were talking about.

"So someone here takes these girls to the Cities and sells them for sex? I don't get it? Why wouldn't they run away, come back home?"

"Well, I don't think they have much choice, Cash. Maybe they trusted the wrong person. That person takes them down to the Cities and gives them to a guy called a pimp. The pimp keeps them drugged or locked up. And they're forced to have sex with men. Pretty soon, maybe they're too ashamed to come back home. I've heard rumors of it but never actually seen it happen, so it might just be a far-fetched idea the guy you know is talking about."

"Everyone is having sex with everyone, Wheaton. Free love and all that." She raised her voice. "Why are people paying for sex?"

Wheaton blushed. Looked over at the waitress who was clearly pretending to read the newspaper.

"I don't know how to explain it to you, Cash. There are people out there who aren't very nice."

"I know that. But buy sex?"

"It's just a story, Cash. Your friend doesn't know what he's talking about. Eat your pie."

"I did."

"Have another."

"No."

Cash could tell Wheaton was too embarrassed to continue answering questions about prostitutes so she switched gears. "There is another girl missing, Wheaton. Maybe you should go talk to that county sheriff and see what he knows."

"I could call down there. Be quicker than driving. Where did you say? Melon?"

"M-i-l-a-n is how it's spelled and it's south of F-M, close to the South Dakota border."

Wheaton pulled a pen out of his shirt pocket and wrote Milan on his napkin, then stuffed the pen and the note back into the pocket.

"How's school?"

"Good."

"Your grades?"

"Good as gold. Good as gold." Cash smiled, proud of herself. "I tested out of English 101. I don't have to sit through that boring class ever again."

"They let you test out?"

"Yeah. Pretty cool, huh? No sense wasting my time on things I already know. I took the test to get out of science too, but I haven't heard back whether I passed that one or not."

Wheaton nodded, clearly pleased with her.

"New friends?"

"I went to the Indian students' meeting tonight before I came to the game. The counselor fed us. Everyone brought something to eat. I didn't know what to bring—I can't cook—so I just brought cookies. Only got one. Everyone scarfed them down before I could get more."

"Well, good, college isn't just about going to classes. It's meeting new people. Getting new ideas, experiencing and learning things you wouldn't otherwise know about. There's more to life than working fields."

"Prostitution?" Cash couldn't resist asking.

"Nah." Wheaton looked quickly over at the waitress, embarrassed again. "With a college degree, you can see the world. Not be stuck in some little town like Twin Valley here, eating pie and talking crimes with an old man, just passing time. You can see the world. Maybe go overseas. Go to Europe."

Now it was Cash's turn to squirm. She had no desire to leave the safety of the Valley, the life she knew. The steady change of seasons, the planting and growing of one crop after the other, the easy friendships she had with the guys she worked with, the guys who treated her as one of them. They didn't make any demands on her other than that she show up on time and work as hard as they worked. Get as dirty in the fields as they got. She liked shooting pool. Drinking beer. It was the world she had grown up in.

And after the constant change of homes, after the years of abuse and loneliness, the steady rhythm of life in the Valley was all she needed. She didn't need to know if the Cities existed. She was content imagining them in her mind like Superman's Metropolis. *Shoot.* She hadn't told Wheaton about the writing award.

Hanging her head, hands cupped around the coffee cup in front of her, she said in a lowered voice, "I got nominated for some state award."

"What?"

"When I was testing out of English, I had to write an essay. The professor turned it into some award thing and I guess I'm a finalist to get it. I'm supposed to meet him next Saturday and go down to the Cities."

Wheaton smiled. Cash had never seen him look so happy. In his job as county sheriff, he always looked busy. Or concerned. Even when he was off duty. There were permanent horizontal worry lines between his eyes. Always looking out for the next incident, the next speeder, the next kid in trouble.

Now he just grinned at her. "I knew it. I knew it."
The waitress pretended not to look up.

Now it was Cash's turn to blush. "It was nothing. I just wrote what I thought. Something about Shakespeare and Langston Hughes."

"I've heard of Shakespeare but not that Hughes guy."

"About a poem of his I like."

"And?"

"Nothin'. It's nothing. The English professor wants me to go to the Cities. I don't want to ride with him. He might try to sell me into prostitution." Cash smirked.

"Don't be silly. This is a good thing. Of course, you have to go. You could drive yourself down, right? Or take the train."

"That's what I told him, that I'd drive. Take the train? The only time I ever was on a train was one time with the social worker. She took me up to Crookston for a chest X-ray. Did you know my mom had TB?"

Wheaton ignored her question.

"Well, the train goes to the Cities too."

"I'll drive."

"A lot more traffic than around these parts."

"That's okay. I'll figure it out."

"I'm proud of you, Cash."

"Let's go. Your dog is probably eating the left slipper right now."

Wheaton laughed. He pushed himself out of the booth and went up to the waitress and handed her some bills. Cash waited by the door. Watched a car drive by, its headlights reflected on the shop windows across the street. She could also see herself mirrored in the door and Wheaton as he turned from the waitress. He stopped to get a toothpick. He put it in his mouth, something to chew on. Cash opened the door and stepped outside. When Wheaton got to his cruiser, he stood with the door open and said again, "I'm proud of you, Cash. Real proud."

"Probably get some frost tonight," Cash said. She hopped into the Ranchero before he could say anything else. She waited until he backed the cruiser out and turned to head for Ada before she followed him.

When they got to Ada, Cash flicked her brights once at Wheaton to say goodnight. She didn't like drinking in the bars in Ada. They seemed to be frequented by boys she had gone to school with who were now men who had inherited their daddy's farms. By this time of the night Arnie's in Halstad would be slow, the only folks left in the bar would be the old-time bachelor farmers who had no one to go home to.

She drove the forty-three miles to Fargo and pulled in front of the Casbah just short of closing time. Her body relaxed. The blinking Hamm's beer and Grain-belt signs in the Casbah's window looked like fine art to her. She could hear the twang of an old country-western song being played on the jukebox inside. George Jones was rock-a-billying the joys of white lightning: *shhhhh—white lightning*. She breathed in the crisp fall air.

Home, she thought to herself as she pushed open the door. The smell of stale beer and cigarettes imme-diately calmed her nerves. After driving beet truck for weeks, after days sitting in hard desks at school, Cash was happy to be in her element.

Shorty reached under the bar and set two bottles of Budweiser on the wooden bar. Longtime barstool warmers, brothers Ole and Carl, tipped their frothy beer glasses in her direction. Ol' Man Willie was slumped over a half-finished glass of beer in the back booth, a cigarette burning in the ashtray, the smoke surrounded his greasy head like a broken halo.

At the pool tables she saw her brother, Mo, playing against Jim, her tournament partner—maybe now her

ex-tournament partner since she'd been 86'd from
the Flame. Mo was dressed in Army fatigues, Jim
in regular farmer gear: blue jeans and a blue plaid
flannel shirt. Mo was short and wiry, his movements
spring-action taut. Jim, in contrast, lumbered around
the table, farmer slow and plodding. And Jim wasn't
a lumbering type of guy—he was also on the thin side,
but compared to Mo, he moved like molasses that had
been stored in the refrigerator.

Cash stood at the bar watching them before she
moved over and set her beers in the booth, her cigarette
in the ashtray. She put some quarters on the table. "I'll
play the winner."

There was a hoot of *Watch out, boys* from over by
the bar. Mo beat Jim. Cash inserted her quarters and
racked up for a game. Mo showed no mercy and ran
the table. Some of his shots were smooth and easy,
others just jagged-luck shots. The most impressive
ones were shots where the cue ball glided in slow
motion across the green and, without a sound, nicked
a ball—just enough—to send it dropping soundlessly
into a pocket. Cash had shot a lot of pool, watched
a lot of games, heck, won a lot of bar tournaments,
but she had never seen someone cut shots the way Mo
was doing. When he sank the 8-ball, calling last pocket

even though he didn't need to, Cash just shook her head in amazement.

"Well, that was some beaucoup luck," he said, killing a beer. Wiping his mouth with the back of his hand, he asked, "Rack 'em up. Who's next?" looking around at the folks gathered around the pool table. "Who wants to play partners against my sister and me? Don't be shy, that was just some crazy luck there."

Jim pointed his cue at one of the other regulars and pushed his quarters into the pool table. Mo motioned for Cash to break. She used a bar cue and then switched to her own stick after a solid dropped. She made two more balls before scratching on a side pocket shot. Mo draped an arm over her shoulders and said quietly, "If you can see the pocket anywhere behind a ball, you can cut it in. Don't try doing a straight in. You do that, you scratch like you did. Cut it in and the ball won't follow it. Hit it soft. Just graze it."

They played partners 'til closing time. The games were fast. No one in the bar, not even Jim and his partner, were up to taking on the Cash and Mo team. The guys playing them would only play for beers no matter how bad Mo teased them, trying to get them to play for dollars.

When Shorty called, "Closing time. Drink it up,"

Cash and Mo had four beers each lined up on the booth table. And that didn't include the ones they were drinking. Cash gave one to Jim and the other two to Ole and Carl. She watched in amazement as Mo drank two and tucked one in the back of his jeans, the bulge of it covered by the flak jacket he was wearing. The other he tucked in an inside pocket of the jacket. As Cash was putting away her cue, he said, "I'm gonna go drive around. See you back at the pad."

Cash left with Jim tagging behind. "I'll meet you at the apartment." He tapped her shoulder gently. Cash drove her Ranchero around the block and into the parking spot in front of her place. By the time she opened the door, Jim was pulling up beside her. They climbed the wooden stairs, feet clomping simultaneously, the dull *thud* echoing down the street.

CASH FLIPPED ON THE KITCHEN light. Jim looked around as if he'd never seen the place. He eyed Mo's makeshift bed on the floor. A neat pile of Army green. He flicked open the sheet hanging across the room where Cash slept. He looked at her. Cash shrugged and got two beers out of the fridge, handed one to him and popped the top on the other. She undressed quickly and crawled between the sheets, plumping the pillows behind her back so she could sit up, drink her beer and have a cigarette.

Jim came in. He sat cautiously on the bed, drinking his beer, staring at the sheet hanging over the doorway. "How long is your brother staying?"

"I don't know."

"When's he coming back tonight?"

"I don't know."

Cash snuggled down into the bed, curving her body around Jim's skinny back. "Get undressed. Come on. What are you waiting for?"

Jim swigged beer.

"What if he comes back?"

"I imagine he is. You better hurry." Cash snuggled closer, lifting up the back of Jim's shirt, running her hand up his spine.

"Uh, I don't know. Just don't feel right. What if he walks in on us?"

Cash pushed away, almost shoving Jim off the bed. He quickly scooted back on the mattress and took another drink of beer.

Cash sat back up against the headboard, pulling the sheet up to cover her breasts. "Doesn't feel right?" she asked, taking a swig of beer. "I have a brother sleeping on my kitchen floor, a brother I haven't seen in years, and it doesn't feel right?"

"What if he walks in on us?"

"Better him than your wife," Cash responded sarcastically, finishing her beer and throwing herself back down under the covers, pulling them tight up under her chin. "Lock the door on your way out. Don't let the screen door hit your ass."

"Ah, Cash, come on. Don't be like that." Jim leaned over her, kissing her hairline.

"Go on. Leave. Before you really piss me off. Go on!" Cash pulled the pillow over her head. Jim shifted on the bed, took a drink of his beer. Set the bottle on the dresser. The bed creaked as he stood up. Cash could feel him looking at her.

"I'm sorry, Cash. Just makes me uncomfortable. Maybe see you tomorrow night at the bar?"

No answer.

Jim went out the front door, pulled it shut behind him, thudded down the stairs. He started up his truck. She threw the pillow off her head and got out of bed naked. She peeked out of the makeshift curtain, then stepped into the kitchen and grabbed another beer out of the fridge. She crawled back into bed, lit a cigarette, shut off the lamp. In the dark she drank and smoked two cigarettes. She smashed out the last butt, took the last drink of beer, and lay down. Then quickly jumped up, felt around in the dark through a pile of clothes on the floor. She pulled on the closest T-shirt and undies she could find and crawled back into bed. *Damn brother, ruining my sex life*, were her last thoughts as she drifted off.

CASH PULLED HERSELF UP AND out of her window. Her heart beat in her ears and shivered uncontrollably. Her eyes darted left and right as she ran barefoot across the dump ground. She reached the plowed field. Her foot sank into the cold, damp dirt. When she tried to pull her foot up, her front leg sank into the cold, damp dirt. When she tried to pull her foot up, her front leg sank farther into the earth. She threw herself forward, clawing with bare hands, bearing the heavy, labored breathing of the person chasing her. Fear forced her from her body so that she was soon flying above herself. She looked down to see her body stretched out in the mud below, buried to her knees, arms flailing, hair catching in her hands. Instantly, the body in the field changed from herself struggling to two paler, longer-legged, blond women. The young women looked up at Cash. They mouthed, "Help me. Help me."

SHE JERKED UP. MO STOOD at the end of her bed. His hair was disheveled, his face contorted in pain. Cash glanced over at her bedroom window, which was wide open, the screen ripped. She looked back at Mo. He was holding what looked like a broom handle sharpened into a spear. From the streetlight shining in the window, Cash could see a dark liquid on the end of it.

She jumped out of bed, frantic to find the jeans she knew were on the floor. "What the hell have you done?" she asked. "Did you kill someone?"

Mo looked at the spear. His entire body was trembling. "No, I ran into an ambush. They stabbed me in the leg with this punji stick. I fought them off. Took the damn thing away from them. The perimeter is safe. I crawled the wall rather than risk leading them in the front way."

Cash reached behind her toward the lamp. With catlike reflexes he jumped her, pinning her to the floor. "Don't," he hissed. "Don't give away our position."

Cash was scared. She didn't move. He had stopped shaking. He was holding her down, but it was as if he was providing her coverage. He kept shushing her. Finally he rolled off her, soundlessly, and belly crawled under the sheet into the kitchen. Cash lay still, afraid to move. She had heard stories of vets coming back and entering this dark zone. Clearly, she was in the middle of a trip back to 'Nam.

Mo came crawling back. Sidled over to the window, stood, favoring his left leg, which Cash could see was bleeding. He peered out, standing flat against the wall. The punji stick was stuck in his waistband like a sword. With only his one arm visible, he reached out and closed the window as quietly as possible. He pulled the thin curtains firmly shut against the street-light's glare. He hung some shirts over the curtains, shutting out even more of the light, never putting his body fully in front of the window. When light still shone through, he silently pulled the top blanket off her bed and used it to cover the window fully. Cash rolled over and crawled on her belly closer to him. "Mo, you're injured," she whispered. "You need a medic."

He looked at her blankly. "I am the medic of this squad."

"Well, why don't you let me fix you up? No good having an injured medic."

Mo sat down heavily in the stuffed chair Cash used as a dresser/laundry basket. "Only the good die young, soldier. You ain't gotta worry about me."

He pulled one of Cash's T-shirts out from under himself and ripped it, barehanded. Then tore it into narrow strips. In the dark, he wrapped the cloth strips around his leg, across the gash, across the tear clearly visible in his green Army pants.

And he began talking, sitting in the overstuffed chair, brandishing the broomstick punji stick whenever a car drove by. He rambled about the Viet Cong and his buddy still out on patrol. Cash lay on the floor, afraid to move. He didn't really know her.

She didn't really know him. What if his mind shifted gears and started to think she was the enemy? When he reached behind his ear and pulled out a joint, she didn't say a word. The pungent smoke filled the small room. She said a soft *no* when he offered her a toke. She rolled on her side and leaned up to try to get a look at the clock on the dresser. It might have said 4:30. She said quietly, "How about if I crawl out there and bring you back a beer?"

"Good thinkin', soldier. I'll take point. You follow."

He crushed the roach out with his bare fingers and dropped to the floor to belly crawl to the doorway. He peered under the sheet, looking left and right, then signaled with his right hand for Cash to crawl forward. Cash mimicked his forearm, forearm, hip-slide, hip-slide crawl to the fridge. Once there, she hesitated, remembering that when she opened the door the light would come on. She calculated exactly where the beers were in the fridge. In one rapid movement she opened the door, grabbed two beers and shut the door back up.

In that moment, Mo rose from the floor and sprinted across the kitchen to the door leading outside, slid himself upright against the doorframe, blending seamlessly into the wall. He peered out into the night through the door window, punji stick clasped at his side.

Cash belly crawled back into the bedroom as fast as she could, both beers in her hand. Thank god she had a church key on the dresser. She reached up and grabbed it. She opened one beer silently. The second one, the cap flew off and hit the floor on the other side of the room. Mo instantly appeared. He was a silent apparition inside the sheet curtain, a dusky shadow along the doorframe. Cash held the beer bottle up in his direction. He moved soundlessly back to the overstuffed chair and sat down, taking the beer from her outstretched arm on his way. Cash marveled at his quietness.

They drank their beers. Still afraid to move too fast or too far, Cash reached up on the bed and pulled down a pillow and sheet. She wrapped the sheet around her on the cold floor and rested her head on the pillow. She watched Mo light a cigarette one-handed, a move she herself had learned from a Vietnam vet home on furlough. He cupped the cigarette in his hand as he smoked to hide the burning tip. About halfway through, he put the still-lit cigarette between his ring and middle finger at the base of the knuckles. He leaned back on the chair, seemed to be sleeping. After a few moments, with the cigarette burning shorter and shorter, Cash said softly, "Mo?"

"Just checkin' my eyelids for holes, soldier." He stayed completely still.

Cash watched the cigarette burn down to the filter. It was the last thing she remembered as she drifted off to sleep.

SHE WOKE TO THE SMELL of bacon frying. Some guy with a baritone voice was singing. Her brother sang along off-key, *"I'm going home, my tour is done . . ."*

She got up off the cold floor, her legs stiff and cold, and threw the pillow back on the bed and crawled into it, wrapping herself tightly in the sheet. Her blanket still hung over the window.

The baritone sang in measured beats, "*I'm going home, I'm a lucky one . . .*"

"I'm a lucky one," her brother repeated, banging out the beat with a spatula against the metal stove.

Cash pulled the pillow over her head, then threw it and the sheet off. She got up, pulled on her jeans from the night before, lit a cigarette.

Jeezus Christ, what the hell was that? she asked herself, looking around the bedroom. She stood next to the window and looked out. The screen had been cut in half. She opened the window to a blast of frostbite air. She grabbed the window frame, leaned out and looked down. She lived on the second floor. The exterior wall was red brick. She stuck her hand out and felt the bricks. Between the bricks and mortar was barely room for her fingers. *How the hell did he get up here?* She slammed the window shut, shivering. If he scaled the wall, he was a damn monkey.

"What the hell?" is what she said out loud. "Come and get it. Chow time."

Mo was standing at the stove tending bacon, while

eyeing eggs that were being cooked over easy. On a chair next to his makeshift bed was a record player. The singer was saluting the nurses of Vietnam. Mo saw Cash eyeing the record player. "Had it in my car. Thought you wouldn't mind some early morning music. Chow's on." He handed her a plate with bacon and eggs. She noticed a short stack of already buttered toast on the table, which meant that at some point he had bought a toaster. Sure enough, there it was plugged in on the kitchen counter.

He was wearing a pair of blue jeans. She looked over at his stash in the corner. The Army fatigues he had worn last night were folded on his bedroll, the punji stick nowhere in sight. "Guess it was a little crazy in here last night." He sat down and speared his egg, dipping a piece of toast into the runny yolk and shoving it in his mouth, grinning at her.

Cash sat across from him. "How's your leg?" She searched his left hand, the one that had held the burning cigarette last night as he fell asleep.

"Fine. Just a scratch." He dipped more yolk. He caught her looking at his hand. The skin between his two fingers was nicotine-stained. He laughed. "Ah, you don't know that trick? If you're tired, smoke your cigarette between these two fingers. If you doze off, your fingers automatically close around the cigarette. Won't burn your house down."

Cash ate in silence. She got up and poured herself a cup of coffee and sat back down. She didn't know how to address the situation of the night before, so she didn't.

"Jim came up, but he left right away."

"He's not a bad shot."

"Not at all. We've won quite a few tournaments."

"We should head over to the Casbah later and shoot a few games. I'll show you how to work on those cut shots."

Cash sipped her coffee, smoked another cigarette. She got up and went over to the chair where the record player was, the baritone still singing. She picked up the album cover from the floor. *The Ballad of the Green Berets*. Sgt. Barry Sadler singing.

Mo wrung out the dishrag and then flicked it through the air. "Let's go shoot some pool. Day's a' wasting . . . I'll teach you some of my Minnesota Fats billiard skills."

"Lemme brush my hair."

Within minutes they were out the door and down the stairs. They walked the short distance to the Casbah without talking. It was ten in the morning.

MO SPENT THE FIRST HALF of the day schooling Cash on how to cut in any shot on the pool table. The Casbah didn't serve any food so they snacked on peanuts and popcorn from behind the bar in the afternoon. Around 6 P.M. they went back to Cash's place to get her Ranchero and drove over to Shari's Kitchen in Moorhead for a patty melt. The food took the edge off their buzz before they returned to the Casbah for the rest of the evening. Cash, after drinking all day, even with the meal in between, felt definitely buzzed. Mo, on the other hand, functioned like a person drinking water.

By 11 P.M., Cash was using the edge of the pool table to navigate around and missing more shots than she was making. When she scratched on the 8-ball, she said, "Fuck," smacked her cue on the table, quickly unscrewed it and fumbled to put it back in its case.

Mo laughed.

"Can't hang with the big guys, sis?"

Cash shook her head and sunk into the booth. Jim slid in beside her and nuzzled her neck. Cash pushed him away, "Don't. I feel sick."

"Want me to take you home?"

"Maybe. Yeah." She pushed him out of the booth and he pulled her to standing. He grabbed her cue case and put his arm around her waist. She leaned into him.

Back at her apartment, she fell into the bed. Jim pulled off her shoes and socks, rolled her under the covers. "I'm gonna be sick." She jumped off the bed and made it to the toilet before throwing up. Jim handed her a wet washrag.

"Don't look at me," she said. "Get outta here." She threw up again.

She must have passed out briefly. She dry heaved a couple of times and wiped her face with the washrag. Finally, she thought it was safe enough to stand up. She leaned against the bathroom doorframe, put her forehead on the cool wood for just a second before making a beeline for the bedroom. The sheet almost stopped her. She waved her arm to move it out of her way and stumbled. Jim jumped up off a kitchen chair, grabbed her and took her back to the bed. Cash hadn't realized he was still in her apartment. Before she passed through a fog of gray, she sensed more than saw him bring the wastebasket from the kitchen and place it by her bedside.

THE NEXT MORNING SHE WOKE again to the smell of frying bacon, but this time it turned her stomach. She leaned over the bed and retched. Nothing more to throw up. She heard Mo laugh. Sgt. Barry Sadler sang about a badge of courage. She groaned and held her head between her hands.

Mo called out, "Come and get it."

She rolled slowly off the bed. The floor was cool on her bare feet. She was still dressed in the clothes she had worn to the bar the day before. She tugged the T-shirt over her head a little at a time and put a clean one on in its place. She shuffled out to the kitchen. "Coffee, please."

Mo set a cup in front of her. And a plate of eggs and bacon. He had even made pancakes. "Nothing like a little protein to help a hangover. Eat."

Cash drank half her cup of coffee before attempting the eggs. And then she ate gingerly. Small bites. Swallow. Wait. See how the stomach reacted. The more she ate the better she felt. Except her head. She got up and went into the bathroom medicine cabinet and got two aspirin. She swallowed them down with the rest of her coffee. Mo refilled her cup. He was on his second breakfast, this time two pancakes instead of three. Cash looked at his wiry frame and wondered where he put the food. Barry Sadler quit singing. Mo got up and reset the needle. *The Ballad of the Green Beret* began again.

"I talked to Shorty last night. We're going to do an 8-ball tournament at the Casbah this afternoon. Two brackets. Double elimination. Winner takes all. Everyone will put in five bucks to start. Starts at one. Was afraid you weren't gonna wake up in time." He laughed.

"I'm not gonna drink."

"It's Sunday. All they'll serve is 3.2."

"I need a bath."

"Go ahead. I am already shit-shined and polished."

Cash took a long hot bath. Washed her hair in the tub. Dressed in clean clothes. Rinsed out the wastebasket and dumped the water down the toilet. By the time she was done, Mo had the breakfast mess cleaned up. She hadn't even realized her kitchen was a mess until Mo showed up. Everything he did was clean and orderly. Except the ripped screen in her bedroom. Neither had mentioned that little escapade again. Neither probably ever would.

MO WON THE TOURNAMENT. HE stuffed a wad of bills in his flak jacket pocket at the end of the games. Jim came in second. Cash third. There was some light-hearted ribbing about fixing the games, but all the guys paid up willingly. Cash drank pop most of the day. In the early evening she drank a glass of beer from the pitcher on the table. One beer was enough, she told herself. Mo had been drinking steadily all day long, his side bets on the games kept a pitcher of 3.2 on the table at all times. There was never any indication the booze was getting to him. By closing time she had lost track of the number of glasses of beer she had drunk, her one-glass promise quickly forgotten. But she didn't feel drunk. Just buzzed. Easy. Comfortable.

At closing time they said good night to Jim and walked on home, Mo whistling a childhood tune that Cash vaguely remembered. At the apartment, Mo got them each a beer from the fridge, put on Sadler again and dealt a hand of solitaire.

"I have school in the morning. I'm going to have to work all this week 'cause I took the weekend off and I'm taking next weekend off too." Cash sat down across from him.

"What you doing next weekend?"

"Going to the Cities."

Mo whistled. "Gonna be a city girl? How you getting there?"

"Driving the Ranchero."

"You're driving?"

"I know how to drive. Seems like I been driving all my life."

"What's in the Cities?"

"I might get some award for an essay I wrote for English. The professor says there's an award ceremony at one of the colleges down there."

"Things are different in the city."

"I'm not doing anything, just going down and getting the award."

"Lots of people. Cars. First time I went to a city, I got seasick, like carsick. All the movement back and forth, up and down. Got me dizzy."

"Serious?"

"Serious as a motherfucker." He swooped up the cards, clearly having lost, and dealt himself another run. "When you grow up on this prairie where you can see into yesterday *and* tomorrow depending on which direction you look, all them buildings and cars in the city can make you damn sick. Worse than last night." He laughed and put the eight of hearts on the nine of spades. "Maybe you'll see some streetwalkers."

"Streetwalkers?"

"You are a farm girl, aren't you? Streetwalkers. Prostitutes. Maybe you'll see your missing girls.

They've been gone long enough they've probably been turned out by now."

"What are you talking about?"

"What they do is they take these girls, keep them locked up, drug them. Have sex with them. And then *make* them go out on the streets and sell themselves."

"Why don't they just run away?" Cash took a long drag of her cigarette.

"There's a big bad world out there, sis."

"Come on, why don't they just run away?"

"They can't. They're scared. They're drugged. Maybe beat. How did you get out of the foster homes? Did you run away?"

Cash felt a touch of shame. "No. I didn't know how to run. Where to run. All I know is the Valley. Everyone knows everyone. There was no escape."

Mo leaned his chair back on two legs, his right hand holding him steady from the table.

"So how'd you get away? Trust me, I know foster homes aren't no R&R."

"Wheaton. The sheriff. He helped me. Helps me."

"Same with girls sold into white slavery. There's no escape. Unless someone goes in after them. Gets them out. But they move the girls around. If they're from here, by now they're in the Cities or Chicago. Maybe even New York."

"Serious?"

"Serious."

"Well, Wheaton doesn't know where the Tweed girl is. Doesn't sound like the folks down in Milan have found their girl either. If the Cities are that big, how would you go about finding them?"

"I don't know. Never been to the Cities other than on a layover on the way to Fort Bragg. Each city has a district, a part of town, where the pimps tend to run their girls. Guys can just ask around at any gas station and someone will head them in the right direction. Wouldn't be so easy for you, a girl."

"Wheaton doesn't think that's what happened. He told me to just focus on my studies. He wants me to finish college. I gotta get to bed. School. Work. Bed. Probably won't see much of each other this week."

Cash pushed back from the table, grabbed her pack of Marlboros and went to her room. She pulled her clothes off and crawled under the covers. She debated in her mind whether to get up and get her nightly bedtime beer—she was still troubled by getting so sick the night before, not trusting her stomach, even though the beers at the bar hadn't seemed to bother

her. Rather than get back up, she smoked one last cigarette, rolled over and went to sleep to the soft *slap, slap* of the cards being laid down for the solitaire game, Barry Sadler crooning away.

Cash spent the rest of the week going to school and driving truck. Each morning she woke to a breakfast made by Mo. There wasn't another punji stick escapade.

Sharon, dressed in bell-bottom jeans and a thick oversized mohair sweater, informed her on Monday morning that she was going to "just die" of embarrassment. She had gone to Professor Danielson's office on the Friday before dressed in her sheerest hippie shirt. Instead of swooping her in his arms, he had talked her into babysitting his kids so he and his wife could go out for a drink and movie. Shame had forced her to hide out all weekend. "Sorry to have worried you and Chaské."

She apologized for missing the Homecoming game. Cash told her not to worry—she had forgotten all about it too. Had shot pool instead.

That week, because she didn't have to go to English, Cash spent more hours at the rec center to practice cutting balls into side pockets. Her judo improved. And on Wednesday, she found out she had successfully tested out of science. Another hour of pool was added to her school day. It was cheaper to shoot at the rec center on her student ID pass than to pay for a table and drink at the Casbah. By Thursday, Mo joined her at the rec hall.

That same Thursday, Professor LeRoy called her as she was crossing campus. "You're still coming down with me to the Cities to get that award, right? Big honor for you, for the school. I know you're going to place, take one of the top three awards, would hate to disappoint folks around here, not every day the school has an award-winning writer—at the state level, mind you. Makes us all look good—you're on your way to grad school, and you just a freshman, thought about what classes you are taking next? Don't waste that talent."

Cash wasn't used to folks who talked so much. Or so fast. She stood shifting her schoolbooks from one arm to the other, looking toward the rec center where she had been headed. "Yeah."

"Good, good, good, you still planning to drive? Be a lot cheaper for you if you just rode with me in the state car. It's free, you don't even have to pay for gas; the school gives us a credit card for things like this."

"No. I mean, I'm going to drive. I . . ." She couldn't very well say, "I feel trapped if someone else is driving." Or, "If I need to get away, I want my own way out." She didn't trust her words to make sense to most folks.

"Well, suit yourself, just make sure you are here on Saturday morning to follow me down. It's a city, way bigger than this friendly, *ha*, Scandinavian oasis on the prairie, would hate to lose you once we get down there, no way to find each other if you don't know your way around."

Cash nodded and started to walk away.

"Renee," he hollered after her, "there are some other students going down, some science award thing too. Danielson is riding down with two upperclassmen, but if you change your mind and want to ride along instead of drive, there'll still be room."

Now Cash knew for sure she wasn't riding along. She also knew for sure she wasn't telling Sharon what her plans were for the weekend. She waved at LeRoy and moved on to the rec center. She had just racked up a game when Mo sauntered in. "Rack 'em and weep." He went to pick out a house cue. "Straight eight or last pocket?"

"You break. Straight eight. If you leave me a ball, I might have a chance."

They played for a good two hours, both of them in the zone. Mo instructed her on the cut shots. He bought a pitcher of cola from the help desk. The sugary drink was unpleasant to the two players who were used to the fizz of beer. They sipped the pop slowly, the drinks going flat in the glasses they poured.

"I'm gonna go to the Cities this weekend. Get that award. The professor stopped me on the way over here."

"Don't get sold into white slavery."

"I'm not white. Not blond enough." They both laughed.

Off-key, as always, Mo sang, dancing around the pool table, his cue as his dance partner. "Pretty blue eyes, please come out today . . ." He twirled. ". . . my heart skipped a beat."

"That sucked." Laughed Cash. "That really sucked."

"Hurt my feelings."

Mo bowed to his cue.

"Do you really think that's what happened?" asked Cash, leaning over the table, stretching, giving up and reaching under the table for the "idiot cue." This was another skill she was learning in college—how to use the idiot cue.

"Stranger things have happened," Mo answered. He pointed his finger at the exact spot on the 5-ball she needed to hit to get the ball to drop. "Seems pretty far-fetched, but where else are they? They haven't turned up, have they?"

"Maybe they just ran away. It can be pretty boring around here. What's a girl going to do? Get married and have a bunch of kids. If they just came to Fargo–Moorhead, someone would have seen them already."

"So they ran away to the Cities. Or Chicago. Maybe New York."

"Joined the Army."

"Yeah, joined the Army. Became nurses. Might be enough incentive for me to re-up." He started dancing again with his cue.

"Take your shot." Cash pointed at the table with her cue. "Last game. Then I gotta get to class."

Later, as she was leaving her psych class, Mrs. Kills Horses was waiting at the door.

"Congratulations. Professor LeRoy told me about

the state award you're up for. I knew you could get it," she gushed.

"Thank you." Cash tried to brush past her. *Yeah, right, you knew I could get it*. But Mrs. Kills Horses grabbed hold of her arm. "You are going to the Cities, right?"

Cash hated how Mrs. Kills Horses acted like she owned the Native students, and Cash hated being touched. She twisted a little so her arm came loose. She nodded her head yes.

"I am so excited for you. At Macalester College they have an American Indian studies office too. I heard you're going to be staying at the Minority Students' House. You'll get to meet some of their Indian students."

Cash stood still. Clearly, she wasn't going to get away until Mrs. Kills Horses got through with whatever speech she had to give. *How did she know how to find her? She had to have gotten her class schedule from the registrar's office. What did she want?*

Mrs. Kills Horses was digging in her black, fringed leather purse. It had conch shells inlaid with turquoise up and down the purse handle. "Here! This is the name of the advisor to Indian students at that college. Be sure and look her up. And here is the address to the

Minority Students' Center, the house you'll be staying at. Men tend to forget those kinds of details. If you had told me this wonderful news, I would have been able to drive you down."

Cash took the sheet of paper and stuck it in her back pocket.

"Oh, and one more thing. You know how we talked in the meeting about inviting AIM up? This paper has the address for the AIM office in St. Paul. Maybe you could stop by there and feel it out? See if they would think about coming up?"

"I don't know anyone there."

"Oh, I'm sure that doesn't matter. They'll all be friendly. It's all for the cause. The Native American cause," she said, wholeheartedly, flipping her one braid back over her shoulder and zipping her purse shut. "Just stop by and ask if they would come. We have a tiny bit of money we could give them for their trouble." She turned and walked away, her heels clicking on the granite floor. "Congratulations! Always proud of our shining stars."

Cash stuffed the second piece of paper in her back pocket with the other paper.

She drove to the apartment to get a Thermos of coffee and a tuna sandwich. Mo was nowhere in sight.

Cash drove north of town and started driving beet truck early so she was done by 11 P.M. She stopped at the Casbah, but all the regulars were over at the Flame for the monthly tournament. She played a few games, drank a few beers, danced a few country two-steps with a drunken farmer who only stepped on her toes three times and left the bar at closing time.

She took a quick bath when she got home. Washed her hair in the kitchen sink. Pulled on a pair of jeans and an extra-large T-shirt. Grabbed a paper bag from under the sink and went into her bedroom and looked at her stack of clothes on the overstuffed chair. What did one wear to get an award? *Crap, what if I'm supposed to wear a dress?* She sank down on the edge of her bed and looked at her pile of jeans and T-shirts. Not a dress or skirt in the pile. And it was late. Nothing open. No place to buy a dress in the entire town.

She couldn't even remember the last time she'd worn a dress. Sometime back in, maybe, tenth grade? There was some kind of family reunion for the foster family that everyone got dressed up for. The foster mother insisted that Cash wear a dress. The mother had bought it at the clothing store in Ada. It was a size too big. "You'll grow into it" was a too-often-heard refrain. No one seemed to notice that Cash had stopped growing at twelve. It had been a putrid yellow with a white collar. Cash had "accidentally" washed it in a washer load of bleached clothes. No one was ever going to wear that dress again.

She looked at her pile of clothes and wondered what the heck to take to the Cities.

After fifteen minutes of staring and half a bottle of beer, she dug through the dresser drawers where she kept the clothes and odds and ends she never used. From the bottom drawer she pulled out a long-sleeved cotton shirt she had forgotten she had. It was off-white with tiny blue flowers on it. It wasn't too wrinkled. She smoothed the cotton fabric out on the bed. The shirt had all the buttons. If she put her jean jacket on over the shirt, no one would notice the wrinkles. She rolled the shirt up tightly and put it in the bottom of the paper bag. She found a pair of black jeans and did the same. A pair of undies. A clean bra. Socks. On top of it all, she put in her well-worn cowboy boots. Bottoms up.

There. She was packed. She opened the top dresser drawer and grabbed a couple packs of Marlboros from the carton she kept there. Threw them into the bag. And her hairbrush.

Cash had an internal alarm clock from working

farm labor. Whether she got to bed at 4 A.M. or got drunk the night before or was sick in bed with the flu, she invariably woke up with the sun, daylight saving time or not. Didn't matter. But she was nervous about this drive to the Cities. About this award thing. So she set her alarm for 6:30, just in case. Then she pulled off her jeans and crawled into bed.

As she was falling off to sleep, she thought about the days in foster care. The nights when she would go to bed hoping she wouldn't wake up, or that, if she did, it would have all been a bad dream. There was nothing in her world that had prepared her for college or awards or drives to the Cities. Long ago, she had given up thinking about tomorrow. There was only this moment, this time, this now. With that thought, she was sound asleep.

HER DREAMS WERE DISJOINTED. GIRLS with very long legs, legs as long as electric poles, walked down a street barely lit by streetlamps. Mo danced with a cue stick, but he was doing a jitterbug, not a slow waltz, the cue stick flying through the air. Cash found herself flying over treetops, plowed fields and eventually square blocks of buildings, higher above the ground than any she had ever seen. The air was thick, dense. She had to work to fly through it, not like the country air she was used to flying through in her dreams. She flew for a long time over buildings and more buildings. Looking down, she saw lots of trees, all of them getting winter-bare already. There were lakes and a river winding between two cities, much like Fargo–Moorhead looked from above. The streets were in squares, like farmland, but much, much smaller. She felt a current pulling her to the east side of the river. It was like a gentle vacuum pulling her in and down. She felt her stomach grazing the treetops and she had to navigate her body to miss the upper branches.

She looked down. Below her now were tree-lined streets, with brick and wood houses lining the blocks. There were green street signs on each corner. Cash tried to read them as she drifted by. Selby, Marshall, Kent, Mackubin. Some of the signs were blurred and she couldn't read them fast enough. In midair, she came to a full stop floating in front of a big red brick house. Dark. The street ran south to north. The number on the house was glowing in puke green numbers: 175. This spot was ice-cold. The house had a porch with latticework around the base, one end of which was half torn off. Without waking, Cash rolled over in bed, tightened the covers around her and drifted into a dream about sitting in a truck waiting for a combine to reach her end of the field.

CASH WOKE—ONCE AGAIN—TO THE SMELL of cooking bacon. How in the heck did this guy drink all night, wake up without a hangover and be all cheery and happy cooking breakfast? And what had triggered the flashback the other night?

Maybe he didn't sleep. Or maybe he slept during the day while she was at school or working.

She tore a page out of one of her notebooks, smoothed it out on top of her dresser and wrote down as much of her dream as she could remember. She underscored the number 175.

She rummaged around and found the addresses for the AIM office and the Minority Students' House in St. Paul and put those notes with the paper about the dream on top of the dresser. Then she put on clean jeans and T-shirt with a jean jacket on top of a fleece hoodie to keep her warm.

She stopped, stood momentarily in her room. She wondered if the Cities were far enough south that it might be a bit warmer there than in Fargo–Moorhead.

Two hundred fifty miles probably was not enough to make a considerable difference.

Was there a real Grain Exchange building in Minneapolis? Every day the radio issued the farm market report out of the Grain Exchange. It had never occurred to her before to wonder if it was an actual building.

"Git while the gittin's good, girl," Mo said, putting a plate with eggs, bacon and pancakes on the table.

Cash pulled out a chair and sat down to eat. "Soon my jeans aren't gonna fit."

"You need some meat on your bones. What time you supposed to be over at the school?"

"Ten in the parking lot, where they have the state cars. There's another teacher taking some science students down too. I'll just follow them."

Cash finished eating, put her plate in the sink, stood looking around the kitchen as if she would never see it again.

"Go on. Have fun. This is a good thing."

"You think so?"

"Beat it. I'll guard the home front. See you on the flipside."

Cash went to the fridge and pulled out two beers. "Just in case," she said, when Mo raised an eyebrow.

At the college, LeRoy was already in the parking

lot. So was Danielson and two brainy-looking guys, each wearing a white shirt under a dark cardigan and corduroy pants. They were also wearing hip-length, lined trench coats. They looked like teenybopper versions of college professors. Their hair was thicker and adolescent pimples were still on their faces, but someday they would replace LeRoy and Danielson.

After brief introductions of names Cash forgot as soon as she heard—the Mikes and Steves of the Valley all blended together in her eyes—LeRoy laid out a map on the hood of the state vehicle. He pointed out the roads they would take. "We'll take the new highway as far as it goes, then, here, we'll jump over to old 52, maybe we'll stop in Alexandria for lunch, grab a quick sandwich at the truck stop. Once we're in the Cities, stick close to me, don't let another car get between us; if we get separated, we'll never find each other. Here, you take the map, here's a blow-up of the St. Paul streets in this corner of the map—I've circled the streets where Macalester is, over in St. Paul."

Cash reached back to touch the pocket where she had put the addresses from Mrs. Kills Horses. *Damn*! She'd left the pieces of paper at the house.

"This X is where the Minority House is, but just follow me; I have to drop these guys off at the Sigma

Phi fraternity house where they'll be staying." He folded the map so the roads he had pointed out were showing and handed it to Cash. "Let's go!" All the men piled into the navy-blue sedan with the State of Minnesota license plates. Cash hopped into her Ranchero.

There was little traffic at this hour on Saturday morning. Farmers tended to start their days early, even their shopping days, so anyone who was coming into town was already in town. Plus, most of them would stay for lunch, "make a day of it," at one of the local restaurants.

Cash stayed two car lengths behind the state sedan. Close enough so no one was going to jump in between them. Dean LeRoy was driving the speed limit. Cash turned on the radio.

A lonely country love song drifted from the speakers. She cracked the window two inches and lit a cigarette. Took a sip of coffee from the Thermos Mo had handed her as she walked out the door.

Flat farmland slid by outside. Plowed fields, black dirt waiting for white snow. Golden stubble fields that the deer seemed to love to graze early morning and at dusk. In some fields there was a lonely stand of oak or pine trees. Tall grass grew at the bottom of their trunks, holdovers from early homesteads left behind when families moved to a different quarter-acre to build their new modern, ranch-style homes—families who were more interested in the two-parent household and raising children with TVs, phones and modern ideas. They left Ma and Pa behind to live out their final years on the old farmstead with their old-world ideas. Most of those houses were now a pile of timber hidden by the tall grass and tree trunks.

About forty miles out of town, the landscape changed. Flat land gave way to rolling hills. Cow pasture, where Angus or Hereford cows grazed, co-existed with corn stubble and plowed soybean fields.

The little college caravan had reached the edge of Lake Agassiz. The lake, the result of a melting glacier moving north, had existed for over ten thousand years. The glacier had shaved the land flat, leaving behind the Red River and the surrounding Valley. The yearly flooding of the river, caused by the abundant snowfalls of the north and the multiple small creeks and rivers that overfilled their banks with the freezing spring melt off, created the thick rich topsoil of the Valley.

Black gold is what the area farmers called that soil. They would stand around in their fields in the summer and fall months, kicking clumps of dirt. Or bend down to crush the soil between their calloused hands. The richest dirt was pitch black and fine. Closer to the river, it began to mix with river clay, causing slippery roads for truck drivers hauling beets or potatoes to the harvest plants. On the highway where Cash was driving now—on a slight, barely perceptible incline—she entered the upper ledges of what used to be that ancient lake.

Up here, the soil contained sand. Kids would sometimes dig through the fields, ditches and farmyards to find seashell fossils. In the spring, farmers harvested rocks on the edge of Lake Agassiz. In the Minnesota winters, the ground would freeze up to four feet below the surface. When it warmed in the spring, rocks were pushed to the top. On the lake edge, now turned to farmland or left as oak and pine forest, abandoned farmsteads often had a pile of boulders in addition to the falling down buildings of the ancestors. Teens from the Valley hired themselves out in the spring to walk the fields and toss rocks into a wagon driven beside them. It was a job Cash herself had never had to consider. Driving truck was her primary trade.

The land rolled by. The hills were so different from the flatness of the Valley. You really could see forever in the Valley. On the horizon at home the only thing that might block the view were the oak and cotton-wood trees that snaked along the Red River.

Cash saw the sedan's right blinker flick on. She followed the car off the interstate and pulled into a gravel parking lot. A Standard Oil gas station sat next to a low-slung building, a truck stop proclaiming HOME-COOKED MEALS. Cash got out and followed the guys into the restaurant. Truckers sat slumped at the counter, drinking coffee and smoking cigarettes, tapping the ashes into black plastic ashtrays set between each stool. Others were eating pie or finishing a roast beef sandwich smothered in gravy. No one looked up when they entered.

LeRoy and Danielson led the students to a table looking out the large glass window, their view the gravel lot and other cars being waited on by pump attendants in dark blue Standard Oil uniforms.

"You kids get something to eat. We'll put it on the college credit card. Sandwich and a piece of pie might hold you until we eat tonight," LeRoy said as the waitress handed them each a plastic-covered menu and, without asking, poured everyone a cup of coffee.

Cash knew enough not to turn down a free meal and ordered the hot roast beef sandwich and a piece of apple pie. Danielson seemed to be on his good behavior, his leering and over-friendliness put on hold. The men—the teachers and students—talked about fertilizer and hybrid soybeans, which is what the guys' science project was about. Cash wished she had the nerve to ask them if they knew where the Grain Exchange building was. But, because she didn't know if it was a real place or just a radio show, she kept eating her lunch.

After a brief mention of Cash's writing award, she was ignored for the rest of the meal. Sometimes she would look up and catch Danielson looking at her, but not in the overt flirting way he did with Sharon and her back at campus. It was a more calculating look.

When Cash was finished, she excused herself and went to the bathroom. When she came out, the men were bunched around the cash register as if all of them were paying the bill. Cash stepped outside and lit a cigarette. The sun was shining and the air smelled of gasoline and diesel fuel.

Without saying a word, the guys came out and piled back into the sedan. Cash got in the Ranchero and followed the car out of the parking lot and back onto the freeway. After a quick glance at the map, she figured they were about halfway to the Cities. What would that be like? Her stomach fluttered. Maybe

Superman would fly down and greet her. She wondered how to find out where the Grain Exchange was, if it really existed.

She turned up Hank Williams. When she found herself singing along, she laughed out loud remembering Mo's off-key renditions of every song he sang. He seemed to know the words to them all too, and he didn't seem to care that he sounded so bad.

As they got closer to the Cities, there were more towns along the road, especially after they left 94 and got on 52. Highway signs declared eighteen miles—ten miles—next exit Minneapolis. As they got farther into the main city, she recognized the Foshay Tower from pictures in the newspaper and schoolbooks, the word Foshay in tall black letters, clearly visible embedded in the brick top.

Leaving Minneapolis, they crossed a bridge over the Mississippi River. Another highway sign told them they were now in St. Paul. They exited the freeway onto tree-lined streets. They were bare of leaves now except for a few reluctant hangers-on. Cash squinted her eyes trying to imagine what the city must look like when all the trees had all their leaves.

She imagined a princess's palace, like the pictures in Grimm's *Fairy Tales*. Soon they were driving into a part of the city where the houses did look like castles and the streets were named Grand Avenue and Summit.

And then they arrived at Macalester College. It was a majestic place, more regal than the Moorhead State campus. LeRoy seemed to be driving in circles. Finally he pulled over and parked. He got out of the sedan and walked back to Cash.

"Just follow me and we'll go drop these boys off. It's taking me a bit to find their housing, but shouldn't be too long now."

"Okay."

"Then I'll take you to the Minority House."

Cash nodded. He returned to the sedan. It took another ten minutes to find the boys' housing. Cash waited in the Ranchero, watching well-dressed students walk around the campus. Not as many hippies here, she thought.

With the boys and Danielson deposited, LeRoy led her to a three-story white brick house on the edge of the campus. It had a curved driveway. Cash pulled in behind the state car and waited until LeRoy got out and walked up to the door. He turned around and motioned for her to come over.

Cash didn't know what to do. She had no intention of staying overnight in a house that looked like it belonged in a fairy tale. Since Wheaton got her the apartment, she had never slept anywhere except there or in the bed of her truck. She didn't see that changing tonight. But she didn't want to give that information to Dean LeRoy.

She walked up the brick staircase to an oak door they could have walked through together, side by side, it was that wide. Dean LeRoy rang a bell that Cash hadn't even seen. Every bone and muscle in her body told her to run, and to keep running. But she stood stock-still.

A fashionably dressed black woman in her mid-thirties answered the door. Her hair was styled into a modish Afro. Her navy leather pumps matched the navy skirt she was wearing. Cash had read about silk blouses. The yellow blouse with bright red flowers the woman was wearing was the first one she had seen in real life.

"You must be Renee Blackbear," she said, extending her hand for Cash to shake. Her fingernails were painted a pale pink. "Welcome. Come on in. And you are Professor LeRoy, correct? Pleased to meet you both. Call me Frances," she said to Cash. "I'm the house mother here. Come on in. Let's shut the door—it's a bit chilly out this time of the year."

But Cash felt colder inside than she did standing outside.

"Let me show you around. You can bring your suitcase in and get settled once you know where you'll sleep."

LeRoy excused himself. "I'll be staying at the fraternity house with the others who came down. I'll come back at five-thirty to take Renee to the award ceremony."

Frances fluttered him out the door, assuring him she would make Renee feel right at home. "Come on," she told Cash, "I'll show you where you can sleep. The kitchen is over there. There are probably some chips and such, if you want a midnight snack."

The more silent Cash was, the more talkative Frances became, until she was chattering like it was forty-below.

Frances showed Cash the parlor and the library and another living room. Each of the rooms was decorated with *Black is Beautiful* posters or photographs of Martin Luther King Jr. In one of the side rooms, Cash saw posters of Indian chiefs thumbtacked to the wall. In another room, *the ballroom*, Frances called it, black light posters of Jimi Hendrix and Kool and the Gang were tacked up.

Soon they were back in the wood-paneled front room. Frances's face begged Cash to say something. Cash held up her pointer finger in the universal sign of "just one minute" and she walked out the door. Before she even got one step out, she inhaled and exhaled. Inhaled again. The crisp fall air filled her lungs and refreshed her mind. She dug in her jean jacket pocket and lit up a Marlboro. Just as she threw the match on the ground, the door behind her opened and Frances said, "You'll have to move your truck to the parking lot on the side there." And then she shut the door behind her.

Cash finished her cigarette before she went to her truck to move it. She checked to make sure her .22 was tucked way behind the front seat out of sight. She hadn't fired the rifle since the incident a couple months ago, when two hotheads from Canada had killed an Indian guy who had come down from Red Lake to help with the harvest season. She had stuck her cue stick back there too thinking that maybe, somewhere in the big city, there might be a pool hall she could check out. While she was digging around in the truck and arranging things, she also remembered the money she had stashed in the springs under the driver's seat. She reached up and felt around. Yep, the roll of bills was still stashed between two of the wire springs.

Cash grabbed the paper bag with the clothes she had packed to wear to the award ceremony, locked the truck up and went back into the big house. Frances was sitting on a couch, pretending to read a newspaper. Cash pointed toward the stairs and Frances nodded.

She closed the door to the room.

Everything in the house was thick and dark. Thick wool carpets. Thick brocade curtains. Thick mattresses. Thick walls.

She sat carefully on the edge of the bed. It had one of those nubby bedspreads the foster mothers seemed to love. Cash tugged at one of the small tufts. She remembered picking a bedspread bare in one of the homes, picking the tufts out in her sleep. That had ensured a beating.

She shifted on the bed. She hadn't seen anyone else in the house. Frances had said most of the students who were staying over the weekend were at the football game. There was a clock on the bed stand that said it was 4:30. Dean LeRoy would be by in an hour to get her.

Cash changed clothes. She stood on the edge of the clawfoot bathtub to get a look in the medicine cabinet mirror. With her jean jacket on, the shirt didn't look too wrinkled at all. She stepped down off the edge of the tub and pulled the shirt collar out over the jean jacket collar. There, she almost looked dressed up.

She moved her ID, money and matches into the back pocket of the jeans she was wearing. She rolled up the clothes and the tennis shoes she'd worn down to the Cities and put them in the paper bag, then put on the cowboy boots with her jeans tucked in. She brushed her hair and rebraided it into one long braid. She stood back up on the bathtub edge. Gave herself a once-over. Figured it would have to do.

When she left the house, paper bag in hand, Frances was nowhere to be seen. There were two Indian students sitting side by side on one of the couches, eating potato chips from a green glass bowl. The three of them nodded their heads at each other and said nothing.

She had just stashed the paper bag in the cab of the truck when LeRoy pulled up beside her. Danielson and the boys were in the car with him.

"Ready for your big night?" he asked Cash as all four of them got out of the car. The boys were now wearing suit coats over their cotton shirts and corduroy pants. Each was wearing a square knotted tie around his neck. "We can walk to the banquet center from here. You gonna be warm enough?"

Cash nodded. She'd be fine. She locked up the Ranchero and stuck the keys in her front pocket.

Cash didn't feel so underdressed once she got to the banquet. Some of the women were wearing dresses and heels, their hair in Jackie Kennedy bouffant styles. But plenty of others were dressed in flared bell-bottoms and sheer made-in-India cotton shirts. A few wore thin-braided leather headbands, their long blond hair purposely brushed out to look unkempt. Most of the guys were dressed like the two dudes with her: junior college professors.

The tables were set with white tablecloths, napkins folded like cranes on the top plate. On one side of the plate was a line of forks and on the other side an equal number of spoons. Cash watched carefully as the men at her table navigated the plates and bowls and cups and silverware. The meal was some kind of chicken. The overpowering taste of sage almost made her gag. She filled herself up on mashed potatoes and mixed vegetables as presenters gave short speeches for each category of awards.

Professor LeRoy drummed his fingers on the table as they called out the third and second place writing award winners. When Cash's name, Renee Blackbear, was called for the first-place award, he jumped to his feet clapping furiously. Cash was so nervous she out-of-bodied herself the minute she heard her name. She watched herself get up from her seat at the table, navigate between the tables to the microphone, accept the paper award, shake some hands and move through the tables to sit back down.

As she plopped down on the red velvet chair at the table, she also returned into herself. All of one being, she held the award out and read *Awarded to Renee Blackbear*. As if listening from underwater, she heard Mr. Danielson ask to see the award. He was already reaching out to take it from her. It got passed around the table. All the men offered their congratulations, Professor LeRoy the happiest of all. Cash was still in a fog of tension, repeating *thank you, thank you* to each comment.

God, she wanted a beer. The adults at the table were smoking. In fact, LeRoy was chain-smoking. She looked around and saw that some of the girls dressed in bell-bottoms were smoking at their tables. She lit up.

Talk at the table turned to what each of them wanted to do on Sunday before driving back to Fargo–Moorhead. The boys wanted to visit Como Zoo.

Danielson wanted to stop by Shinder's Bookstore in downtown Minneapolis. Everyone at the table snickered except Cash. She had no idea why visiting a bookstore would cause grown men to snicker until one of the boys said, "You can get me the latest *Playboy*." And the table erupted in laughter. Cash was ignored, as usual—"just one of the guys."

LeRoy asked, "Anything you want to see, Cash?"

Maybe because she was upset at the guys wanting a *Playboy*. Or because she felt totally excluded from the night's festivities and certainly out of her element in this swanky place with white tablecloths, too much silverware and red plush chairs, Cash heard herself saying, "The Grain Exchange."

"The Grain Exchange?" one of the guys said, as if it were a foreign planet. Maybe it was just a word, not a place.

Cash ducked her head, a feeling of shame washing over her. This whole weekend was bringing up feelings of shame—from the fancy Minority Students' House to the dinner of chicken she gagged on. It reminded her of the times in foster homes when she was denied something other folks took as normal: a birthday not celebrated or not getting school pictures. School pictures were a luxury the county never covered for the foster homes. While the other kids traded billfold-size pictures in study hall, Cash would hide in a book, reading to escape the present. Shame was a constant companion.

She had spent the last three or four years living her life so she could escape feeling such shame. She looked up at the men seated around the table. They stared back at her without saying a word. She couldn't tell what they were thinking—if they were laughing at her or judging her. Finally Danielson said, "Shinders is downtown at 7th and Hennepin. I think the Grain Exchange is on 4th and 4th."

One of the boys said, "Yeah, on 4th and 4th. We visited it for our Junior Future Farmers of America class trip. It's pretty noisy with everyone hollering out the stock numbers. I don't know if it's open on Sundays though."

"You can ride with me," said Danielson. "We can go to downtown Minneapolis in the morning and look around."

Over my dead body.

LeRoy said, "I wanted to go see the Cathedral on Summit. I was hoping that you would drive that way with me, Cash. There's a college professor who was one of the judges for the writing award. I'd like to introduce you to him. He was mighty impressed with your work."

"Okay." She jumped at the opportunity to avoid a trip to downtown Minneapolis with Danielson. "In the morning? I think I'll get up early and drive downtown and just walk around outside the Grain Exchange."

"Sure. You can meet me outside the Cathedral after Mass and we'll go to the professor's. He lives up on Summit Hill."

One of the guys, the one who wanted a *Playboy*, nudged the other guy and said, "We'll go to Shinder's with you, Mr. Danielson."

The guys all laughed. Folks began to drift out of the banquet room. The Moorhead State group walked briskly back to the parking lot of the Minority Students' House. The guys said goodnight and hopped into the state car. LeRoy rolled down the car window. "Nine in the morning, outside the Cathedral." Cash waved in agreement.

As soon as they were out of sight, Cash got into the Ranchero and drove toward Minneapolis using the Foshay Tower as her landmark.

She poked along through downtown. Past Shinders on Hennepin. Past a lively bar called Moby Dick's—it looked like a bigger version of the Casbah—but she didn't stop. She drove the length of Hennepin Avenue and then down Nicollet. There were some women in very short miniskirts and beehive hairdos wearing extremely high platform heels. The way they stood, hips or chest jutted out, with their eyes scanning each car that drove by, Cash wondered if they were prostitutes. None of them had long blond hair like the missing girls.

She cruised over to 4th and 4th and parked across the street from what she assumed was the front door of the Grain Exchange. It was a large square building with hundreds of windows up and around the walls. She counted ten floors of windows and ten windows around one side and eight on the other. There were still some lights on in the building, but no one was out walking on these quieter downtown streets.

The Grain Exchange had been a constant part of her life since she first heard the stock report on the radio. If she thought about it, she had probably heard the farm market report every day of her life since she started driving truck.

A couple of cars drove by on the street. The reflection of the red, yellow and green from the stoplights changing signal colors vibrated on the cold pavement. Metropolis was real.

Without thinking, Cash jumped out of the truck, ran across 4th and put a hand against the stone of the building. It was cold. Colder than the night air. Cash shivered, more from excitement than from the cold. She walked past the brass and glass doors and saw men standing around in a large room. The floor was some kind of polished stone with large marble pillars like she had seen in pictures of ancient Rome. The men were talking, using big hand gestures, excited about whatever they were discussing. Cash walked to the end of the block, looking in the windows as best she could.

When she got to the corner of the building, streetlights allowed her to see letters and triangles carved into the stone of the building. She used her finger to trace a triangle. She shivered again. It was beautiful. Cash had had no way of imagining what the Grain Exchange would look like. If anything, she had thought there would be a man sitting at a wooden desk in front of a radio microphone, reading the stock reports from pieces of typing paper.

Peering back in through the large glass windows, Cash saw large boards with numbers written on them, room-sized chalkboards. Each had rows of numbers across and down.

Written with decimal points. She laughed out loud. Not only was the Grain Exchange a real building, but the numbers the announcers read on the radio came from somewhere and apparently had meaning to people besides farmers standing in the field, a smile crossing their faces if wheat was selling for more than a dollar a bushel. A spit in the dirt and a kick of the tractor tire if corn dropped three cents.

Cash ran back across the street and hopped into her truck. She started the motor and turned on the heat. She pulled her jean jacket tight around her as she waited for the cab to heat up. She felt like a little kid on Christmas morning. If someone had asked her why she was so happy she wouldn't have known how to explain the excitement of discovering that things, life, existed outside of the Valley.

She smoked another cigarette while she considered the Grain Exchange, enjoying the discovery of this corner of reality, smiling to herself. When she finally felt fulfilled, had drunk in enough of the structure and stone building, she put the truck in gear and drove slowly away, looking back again and again, as if she was leaving an old friend.

She left downtown Minneapolis and drove University Avenue into St. Paul. She remembered Mrs. Kills Horses telling her to stop in at the AIM office, but she'd left that address lying on top of her dresser back in her apartment. She turned on the radio to find out what time it was. She had to turn the dial to find a station that wasn't all static-y and then wait through a couple of songs before the announcer said, "And the time, in the City of the Lakes, is ten-eleven. Stay tuned for number thirty in our countdown of this week's top hits." Cash turned the radio off. She wanted to soak in all the sights and feelings the city had to offer without any distraction.

She tried to visualize the scrap of paper she'd shoved in her pocket. Maybe it was all the city lights, but she was having a difficult time pulling up the image. As she pulled to a stop at the streetlight at University and Dale, she looked to the left. There stood another bunch of women, high heels, miniskirts, smoking cigarettes, leaning into the open windows of cars that pulled up near the sidewalk. A movie marquee advertised XXX SNOW WHITE AND THE SEVEN DWARFS XXX. By the look of the men sidling into the theater, Cash gathered it wasn't a Walt Disney feature.

At that moment, an unmarked police car ran the red light at the corner, lights flashing, and pulled up to the curb on Dale. The women scattered like birds. Cash sat through the light, watching them run behind buildings and into alleys. Some ran across the street, barely missing moving cars. One woman's blond afro wig flew off her head. Money, bills, flew behind her into the night air as she dipped behind the wooden stairs of a building and got lost in its shadow.

Two guys got out of the car, dressed in street clothes, not cop uniforms. They walked a few feet on each of the street corner sidewalks. One of them cut across the street and started picking up the money blowing around.

"Leave my fucking bread alone, you damn pig."

Cash couldn't see anyone but it sounded like it came from the top of the stairs across the street. The cop laughed, held up the bills he had managed to catch and rifled them, fanning them out.

"Fuck you. Pig."

The cop stuffed the money in his front shirt pocket.

"Come and get it," he hollered up.

"Pig. Fuck you, pig."

He laughed, came back across the street and got into the unmarked car. His partner joined him as the dark sedan, almost the same make and model as the Moorhead State car, drove off.

Cash pulled over next to the curb to get a better view of all the excitement. Gradually women came back out, walked up to each other, and stood in pairs. They complained loudly about the "pigs" ruining their night's work, how they'd have to work overtime to make up the difference. The woman who'd lost her money emerged from the shadows. She picked up her wig and pulled it back onto her head. She bent down to pick up some money the officer had missed, her miniskirt riding high up over her underwear. As she was still squatted down, a car came from the other direction and pulled up next to her, blocking her from Cash's view. Cash saw a man reach over and roll down his window. The woman stood up and leaned in his car. And then she got in the car and they drove off.

Cash thought about what Mo had said, about women being sold on the white slave market. Some of these women were white and some were black. These women looked like girls, looked like they should still be in high school, not walking the streets dressed in short skirts and fake fur jackets. And it didn't seem to Cash as if they were being forced to be out here. She looked up and down trying to see if some menacing guy was watching them, making them stand out here, making them get into the cars with strange men. Cash couldn't see anyone.

At that moment there was a rap on the Ranchero's passenger window. A white man was leaning down, face pressed against the car window. A leer on his face.

Cash heard the passenger door handle click. That was all it took for her to throw the Ranchero into first and get the hell out of there. She ran a red light. Thank god no cars were crossing the street at that second. The adrenaline rush left her shaking.

In two blocks she pulled over to the curb again, reached and pulled the passenger door shut tight and locked it. She lit a cigarette and watched in the rearview mirror just in case the creep had decided to chase her down the street.

Up ahead she saw a small white castle. It had all its lights on and there were people inside. It was called White Castle, a burger joint, it looked like. Still shaking, she pulled in and decided to get a cup of coffee. Something hot to drink might help calm her nerves.

Lone men sat on round stools at a short counter. Five teens huddled around a cigarette machine, three nervously looking around while the other two fed coins into the machine and pulled the knob to get a pack of Camels. A guy behind the counter, wearing a white pointed hat, looked at Cash and asked, "What can I get for you, doll?"

Cash had never been called doll before. This was a night of firsts. "Coffee."

"Black?"

"Yep."

"That'll be a dime."

No one at the counter paid any attention to Cash. In Fargo–Moorhead, everyone, everywhere you went, looked you over. To see if they knew you. To see if they went to high school with you. To see if you were from the neighboring farm. Here, no one looked up from their coffee or burger or newspaper.

Cash took the foam cup from the guy behind the counter and went back out to the Ranchero. She sat there, looking at the men through the car and the White Castle window, all still hunched over the counter. Three white men. Two black men. Each wearing some kind of dark fall coat. Sitting like crows on a barbwire fence.

When the coffee was half gone and lukewarm, Cash remembered Mrs. Kills Horses saying something about the AIM office being in downtown St. Paul in some church. She headed out onto University Avenue.

She continued east on University where she could see the state capitol up ahead. Even in the dark, it glowed white. She got to the capitol and drove around the building. It didn't impress her nearly as much as the Grain Exchange building.

She drove by a Sears building on her way into the main downtown district. As soon as she read the street signs, she remembered a 10 had been written on the note Mrs. Kills Horses had given her. She drove through the downtown streets until she found 10th. Red streetlights caught her at almost every corner, she was driving so slowly. Just when she was ready to give it up, she saw a church a block ahead.

A stoplight caught her at the cross street before the church. As she waited for the light to change, a group of Indians came out of a side door. She could hear their laughter even with her windows rolled up. They split up into pairs and groups of three or four, hopping into beat-up cars that were parked in the church parking lot.

One of the men who had walked out of the church, his arm draped across a short woman's shoulders, was Long Braids. Cash sat through the light again.

Cash had slept with Long Braids a couple of times up north when she was going back and forth between Fargo–Moorhead, Red Lake Reservation and Bemidji, helping catch two guys who had killed a Red Lake man. On his last night in Fargo, Long Braids had spent the night at her apartment. A first. Cash never let anyone spend the entire night in her bed. Never.

That night, they drank beer, slowly, not getting drunk, just drinking. Smoking cigarettes. They laughed and talked until almost five in the morning when both of them finally fell asleep. Three hours later, Long Braids woke, stretched, and stepped out of bed naked to go wash up in the bathroom while Cash made coffee, wrapped in the sheet she had pulled off the bed. From the kitchen she watched him walk back to the bed, pick his clothes up off the floor and get dressed.

He came back to the kitchen table and sat down. They barely talked. Drank their coffee. Looked at each other. Smiled a bit. Finally, when his coffee cup was empty, he stood up. "I gotta go."

Cash hadn't answered. Just stood still, wrapped in the bedsheet.

He'd pulled her into his arms and kissed her. Softly on the lips. Then softly on her forehead. "You'll be my main snag? Okay?" he'd said.

"Okay," she'd replied into his jean jacket.

And he left, neither of them saying goodbye or waving. Cash locked the door and crawled back into bed. Caught unaware, she felt the huge emptiness of all the people who had ever left her. It was the first time in years that she remembered feeling like crying. Instead she went back to sleep.

Now here in St. Paul, at what must surely be the AIM office, she sat through another red light as she watched him climb into a rusted-out Ford. The woman whose shoulders he had his arm across climbed into the front seat first and another woman got in after her. All three in the front seat. Cash watched the car pull out of the parking lot and head up toward the area of the capitol.

Cash threw the Ranchero into drive and turned in the opposite direction. She sped through downtown at least three blocks before she hit the brakes and slowed back down. She lit a cigarette, rolled down the car window, inhaled deeply then blew the smoke out into the night air. She drove around aimlessly for a couple of more cigarettes, radio tuned to a country station. Conway Twitty came on to sing "It's Only Make Believe." She flipped the radio off and gunned the engine. She looked around the streets and saw the cathedral standing guard on a hill over the downtown. She had never seen a building so big, a combination of a medieval castle and some ancient Roman structure. At least she'd know where to come find LeRoy in the morning.

Another streetlight caught her on the cross streets of Western and Selby. As she sat there waiting for the

light, the cab of the Ranchero filled with frigid air.
Canuck winter winds surrounded Cash. The radio
turned itself off. A chill ran up the back of her neck.
Cash looked behind her, first in the rearview mirror.
Nothing. She turned around and looked into the bed
of the Ranchero. Nothing there. As fast as the cold
had filled the cab, it dissipated. The radio came back
on. Conway sang, "You mean more to me than any
other girl."

Cash turned the radio off again. She sped through
the intersection as soon as the light changed. She shook
a bit, a fast shiver, and turned the heat up in the cab.

The next light she got caught was at the intersection
of Selby and Dale. This corner was hopping. Groups of
women, dressed like the ones up on Dale and University, congregated on each corner by the streetlights.
There were men in long coats and fedora-type hats also
strutting around, a certain gait to their walk that said,
"This street belongs to me." There were also more cars
with a single white male in the driver's seat, slouched
low, the body language saying, "Don't look at me,"
all the while their eyes darted hungrily at the women
on the sidewalk. Cash looked to see if the unmarked
police car was anywhere around and didn't see one.

When the light changed, she moved forward slowly,

taking in as much of the night action as she could. This time she had the presence of mind to check the faces of the white girls to see if any of them looked like the pictures she had seen of the Tweed girl or the girl from Milan.

Through the intersection, she pressed her back against the seat and stretched her arms out in front, bracing against the steering wheel. She'd been gripping the steering with her fingers clenched and arm muscles tightened. She wiggled her shoulders and kept driving west.

About a mile down the street, she started to recognize street names that she had seen around the Macalester campus. She turned down one. In a few blocks she saw the tree-lined streets she remembered. She drove around until she passed the Minority House, with still a few lights on.

She parked far away from the house and from the main doorway. She would never be able to sleep there, in a strange bed with strange people in the same house, but she had to sleep somewhere. She turned the heat on high and rummaged around behind the seat until she found the wool blanket she knew was back there. She hated wool. It was scratchy. It reminded her of jailhouses and lost mothers. But tonight she pulled the blanket out and wrapped it around the length of her body. When the cab was too hot for comfort, she turned the engine off and lay down on the seat. It took her a few tries, but eventually she got comfortable with her arms under her head and fell into a deep sleep.

WHEN CASH WOKE UP, HER breath was steamy and matched the gray morning sky. With the blanket wrapped as tightly around her as she could manage, she sat up and started the Ranchero.

She lit a cigarette. The smoke swirled heavily in the truck but she was too cold to roll the window down. After a couple of drags, she cracked the window a quarter of an inch and blew the smoke out as best she could. There was no one else in the parking lot, on the sidewalks or driving on the street. The sun wasn't really up. The half-naked trees foretold winter coming.

Cash needed to pee. She sat in the cab smoking and jiggling her legs. When she finished the cigarette, she shut off the truck and, with the blanket still wrapped tightly around her, jumped out and walked quickly into the Minority House. She opened the door as quietly as she could, peering around in the interior darkness as she moved toward the stairs that led to her bedroom.

As she passed the carpeted living room where she had first met Frances, she could see a couple of students wrapped in each other's arms lying on the brocade couch, one blue-jeaned leg thrown over another. Neither stirred as she snuck past.

Upstairs, she used the bathroom, another round of shivers overtaking her body as her bare butt hit the porcelain toilet seat. She cupped a handful of water to her mouth, swishing it between her teeth, pulling the blanket back around her. Another handful of water quenched her thirst. She leaned against the hot water radiator until its heat seeped through the blanket.

She went to the room she was supposed to have slept in and grabbed both feather pillows off the bed and moved to the four-foot-long iron radiator against the wall, arranging the pillows so she could lie across the radiator, slightly curled up, her blanket hanging over her.

She didn't have a watch or clock, but she knew it was somewhere between 6:30 and 7. If she were on a farm, the roosters would be crowing. The heat from the radiator seeped up through the feather pillows and warmed her right side. Careful, so as not to roll off, she turned over to warm up her left.

She was facing the embossed, wallpapered wall. She traced the soft fuzz of the fleur-de-lis design. She thought back over the drive to the Cities the day before. Her trip to the Grain Exchange. She knew she would never forget the picture of men working inside the glass windows late at night, strange numbers written on the walls. The dinner she wouldn't try to hold on to, though she would tuck the award certificate in her top drawer under her socks for safekeeping. Some part of her knew it was important but with no one to share the good news or its importance, there was an emptiness to the recognition.

The two guys from the college had talked about showing their mom and dad their awards, the pride evident on their faces. Maybe she would show Wheaton. He was the one who told her to go to college, so maybe it would matter to him that she had accomplished something.

Cash rolled over on the pillows so her back could get some warmth. She relived her trip by the AIM office. When her daydream took her to the two women getting into the car with Long Braids, she sat up. Her feet, still in cowboy boots, hit the floor. She caught sight of herself in the mirror on the opposite wall. Her hair, which she had braided the day before in one long braid, now had strands sticking out over her ears and from the part down the middle of her head. She stayed on the radiator while she unbraided it, combed it with her fingers and braided it neat and smooth, while her butt got toasty warm.

She went back to the bathroom and ran steaming hot water. She washed her face and armpits and called it a done deal. She snuck back downstairs to get a clean pair of undies from the bag in the truck and stuffed them in her pants pocket. She threw the wool blanket behind the car seat, hit the door lock and returned to the house.

The couple was still entwined on the couch. Neither had moved an inch. She crept back upstairs and changed underwear, stuffing the ones from the day before into her pocket. Feeling dressed, she went back downstairs to the kitchen, found a small electric coffeepot and some Folgers. The clock over the stove said 7:30. Everything in the building was silent except the occasional clang of the radiators and the hum of the refrigerator. There was an ashtray on the kitchen counter. Cash lit a Marlboro and drank her coffee when it was brewed.

In foster homes, she had learned the skill of rummaging silently through other people's belongings. She dug through the cupboards until she found some Corn Flakes to go with the milk and sugar she'd found. After she ate, she dug around some more until she found a stash of foam cups. She filled two of them with hot coffee and carried them out to the Ranchero. She sat in the cab with the engine running, drinking coffee, until the cab was warm. Then she backed out of the parking lot. At the first stop sign, she remembered to pull her panties from her back pocket and stuff them into the paper bag.

She retraced her drive from the night before until she found University Avenue. The streets were empty. The White Castle was still open with a lone counter worker visible through the windows. On Dale and University the XXX theater sign wasn't blinking and there was no evidence of streetwalkers or unmarked cars. Occasionally she would see a station wagon full of a family, the man wearing a Sunday go-to-church hat and his wife a Jackie Kennedy pillbox. There was no movement at all in downtown St. Paul. The church parking lot of the AIM office was now filled with newer station wagons, in much better shape than the Indian cars from the night before. Cash cruised downtown and up the hill to the cathedral.

She found a parking spot on the street named Selby. She took off her cowboy boots and put on her tennis shoes, her feet tired of being encased in leather. With the motor running, the heat on full blast and the window cracked an inch, Cash smoked Marlboros and listened to a church station that was playing some good gospel music while she waited for LeRoy to come out of the cathedral.

Cash thought about her brother back in her apartment in Fargo, about school and how she really didn't fit in there, about the Indian Students' Association and how they were going to bring AIM to the campus.

A soft tap on the window pulled her out of her reverie. LeRoy, wearing a tweed coat, neck scarf and a felt church hat, stood on the street with two steaming cups in leather-gloved hands. Cash rolled down the window. He handed her one of the cups. "Here, courtesy of the nuns."

Cash blew and took a small sip. It tasted like Folgers that had sat a few too many hours, but it was hot and in the chill October air it hit the spot.

He opened the Ranchero door. "Come on. It's right up the street. We can almost see the professor's house from here. I'm parked three cars ahead of you. Come on, I'll drive and bring you right back here."

Without the time to think or object, Cash got out of the cab and rolled up the truck's window. She locked the door. Professor LeRoy grabbed her elbow with his free hand as if to steer her to the sedan. Cash pulled her elbow close to her body and took a step away from him. She followed him as he walked briskly to the sedan. He got there first and opened the door for her. She slid into the car. It smelled new, some combination of leather and plastic. She took another sip of her coffee. It was still too hot to gulp, but the warmth felt good going down her throat.

LeRoy started the engine and fiddled with the heat. He sat sipping his coffee as the car warmed up. "You should see inside the cathedral. Beautiful stained-glass windows and there are large marble statues of all the saints. Maybe when we get back from the professor's, we can peek in the door and you can see the inside. People come from all over the country to see it."

Cash turned to look at the cathedral with its wide marble steps leading up to arched oak doors with angels and cherubs carved into dark wood. One of the angels flapped her wings and winked at Cash. And then the world turned from fall gray to the fuzz of a TV screen when the antenna needs fixing. Then everything went black.

CASH HEARD VOICES FAR OFF in the distance. Mostly female voices. And then a man's voice. He sounded angry. She tried to sit up, but the room began to spin and she flopped back down. There were no coherent thoughts in her brain. Every time she opened her eyes, the room whirled again and she couldn't make out how many other bodies were in the room. People continued to talk. Some in soft hushed voices, some louder. And the angry man.

She stretched out her leg, trying to find the edge of whatever she was lying on. If she could get a foot on the floor, the world would stop spinning and the TV antenna in her brain would fix itself. A door slammed in a faraway world and the world she was in became quiet, though she sensed there were still people very close.

After an eternity, her foot hit solid ground. She heard a soft laugh that sounded like it came through a cardboard tube, long and fat and slippery. She kept her foot on the ground. After what seemed like an hour of trying, she got her hands up to either side of her head and kept them there. She was able to stop some of the spinning that way. But, when she forced her eyes open, the world moved in waves. After a while, though, she was able to determine that she was on a bed in a room with a few other people. And then the world went black again.

The next time Cash came to, she was lying on the same bed. Her head was pounding, but her thoughts and eyesight were finally clear. She looked toward the window to figure out the time of day. The sky was nighttime black. She turned her focus to the other people in the room. There were five of them, three sitting on oak chairs and the other two sharing a vanity bench. All blond. They looked like a team of heavily made-up cheerleaders. Instead of wool letterman sweaters and pleated skirts, they were wearing sequined mini-dresses. The two on the bench were wearing white go-go boots and the others extremely high platform shoes. Their blond hair was piled high on their heads, heavily ratted and hair sprayed into ridiculous-looking updos. They didn't look any older than fifteen, the lot of them.

The slashes of red lipstick across their mouths made them look like grade-schoolers who had gotten into their mother's makeup. Cash knew the tallest was the

Tweed girl and the scared-looking one wearing a pale blue hotpants outfit had to be the girl from Milan. She wondered where the other three were from.

She rolled over on her side and the bed creaked. The girls all jerked and turned to look at the bedroom door while one of them put her finger to her pursed lips.

Cash joined the girls in a motionless watch of the door. When no one came in, they all seemed to relax a tiny bit. One of the girls lit a cigarette and shared it with the others. Cash felt for the pack of cigarettes that should be in her jean jacket pocket. It was still there. Without creaking the bed again, she got a cigarette out and lit it. She flicked the ashes into her bare palm and then rubbed them into the leg of her jeans.

The girls eyed her. She eyed them back. When Cash's cigarette was down to the filter, one of the girls in go-go boots crept across the floor, stopping just once on a floorboard that squeaked. She took the butt from Cash and dropped it into the ashtray they were all sharing back where she'd been sitting.

Cash had a thousand questions, but it was clear the girls were not given to talking. She looked again out the bedroom window. They were on the second or third floor, judging from the tree branches visible outside. It was night, but Cash had no other judgment about the time. She relaxed into the mattress and listened to the other sounds of the house. Occasionally she could hear a car drive by outside. A downstairs door opened and closed. Muffled male voices could be heard in other parts of the house.

There was another double bed pushed against the far wall, but no one was on it: the girls were all huddled on the chairs and vanity bench. It looked like everyone slept and dressed in here. Clothes and high-heeled shoes were strewn across the floor. The vanity itself was covered with makeup and used tissues. Cash looked at the girls and mouthed silently, "I have to pee."

They all shook their heads no. Cash reached down and unbuttoned the waistband of her jeans. That damn LeRoy must have put something in the cup of coffee he had given her. And here she had been worried about Danielson all this time. *Shit*. Maybe they were all in on this—this must be the white slave market Mo told her about. But shit, she wasn't white. What was she doing here?

Footsteps came up the stairs and passed the bedroom door. The girls didn't move. Cash heard a door open and shut and then a toilet flush. There was a bathroom on this floor. Damn, hearing the toilet flush put her bladder into overdrive. What were they going to do, kill her? Damn, she had to pee. As she heard a door open again, she jumped off the bed and rushed to the door. She twisted the door handle and pulled. Nothing. The door was locked. When she heard the footsteps outside the door get closer, she started to pound on the door. The five girls groaned, a deep collective sigh and pulled closer together. "Hey, I gotta pee," Cash yelled.

The footsteps stopped outside the door. She heard a male laugh and the steps went down the stairs.

Cash turned and looked at the girls. "What, they won't let you pee? Do any of you talk? You're Janet, aren't you?" she asked looking at the Tweed girl.

The girl nodded quickly.

"And you're from Mi-lan, Milan—however you say it, right?" Cash said looking at the youngest of the girls. She too shook her head yes. "So, who are the rest of you?"

No one answered. They looked at each other and at the door.

"Oh, jesus, I gotta pee. What time is it? What day is it?"

One of the girls pushed a three-pound Folgers coffee tin can out from under the vanity.

"What? I'm supposed to pee in that?"

The girls nodded. Cash then noticed a line of coffee tins under the vanity.

"Do any of you talk?"

The girl from Milan whispered, "It's better if we don't. Just pee, we won't look."

And they all turned their heads away or looked down at their knees.

Cash grabbed the coffee can and thanked god it was empty. She moved to the side of the bed away from them and squatted down between the bed and the wall with the window. She looked at them over the bed's mattress. They kept their eyes averted. It took Cash a good minute before she could actually pee. Soon the sound of a stream of urine hitting the bottom of the tin can filled the room. The heat from her piss warmed her butt.

Damn, no toilet paper. She shook her butt back and forth, pulled up her undies and jeans in one swift move, stood up. It was a good thing she only had to pee.

She looked at the girls, wondering what else they'd had to endure. When and how did they eat? They looked clean so they must get to use the bathroom once in a while. What if they needed to do more than just pee?

Cash put the lid back on the coffee tin, then turned and looked out the window. She pulled the yellowed-lace curtains to the side. There was one streetlight down the block a ways. She could see St. Paul Cathedral's dome a few blocks over. The golden sheen of the state capitol was blocked from view. The outside windowsill was brick. Cash leaned her head against the glass and looked at the side of the house as best she could. It looked to be made of brick.

She tried to open the window, but it was nailed shut. She figured it would be. A locked door and nailed window. *Crap*. And she was hungry.

At least that was something Cash knew how to handle. She had spent many days hungry. Foster parents enjoyed using food, or the withholding of it, as punishment. She could go days without eating if she had to. She looked around the room. There were cups and glasses sitting on the vanity and floor. The girls saw her eyeing the cups. One of them reached back to the vanity and held a glass of water out to her. Cash walked over and took a couple of small sips. Enough to quench her thirst but not enough to empty the glass. Then she sat back down on the bed.

The girls were dressed like the women she had seen working the streets down on Dale and University. But those were older women. Those women seemed comfortable in their skimpy clothes, high heels and talked loudly and boldly—to each other, the men in the cars and even the undercover cops. These five girls were half-naked and terrified.

They reminded her of herself in one of the foster homes early on. In that home, the mother always found a reason at the end of the day to have the foster father whip her with his leather belt. Over a dinner of roast beef and mashed potatoes, the mother would give a litany of wrongs Cash had committed during the day. She had sassed back. She had used up toilet paper in the bathroom and hadn't replaced the roll. She had given the foster mother a "look that could kill." It didn't matter if the accusations were true or not. By the end of the meal, the father was worked up into a wrath.

After a few months, Cash found herself hunching

over at the dinner table. Her body flinched at any movement either parent made. If they passed her the mashed potatoes, she flinched.

If they walked behind her chair, she automatically curled into herself. The smallest noise made her jump. The mother seemed to get perverse enjoyment when Cash showed any fear. The father whipped her harder when she screamed or cried.

It had taken her years to overcome her body's response to noise and loud voices. She had trained herself to stand completely still in the face of rage or sudden movement, to remain unresponsive, to not even blink.

But these girls had never experienced anything like Cash had gone through. Nothing in their lives had prepared them for what they were now experiencing. When Cash got back up off the bed and walked toward them, they huddled closer together.

"What happens if you make noise? If you talk to each other?" she asked quietly.

"They just want us quiet," one of the girls whispered.

"Do you know what time it is?" Cash asked the group, her voice still lowered.

They shook their head no in unison.

"Seven P.M.? Midnight? Guess."

The Tweed girl whispered, "Maybe two, three in the morning."

"How long have I been here?"

"They brought you in this morning, around noon," another answered.

"Who brought me?"

The girls all shrugged.

"You don't know, or you don't want to say?"

They looked at each other and shrugged again.

"Do you ever get out of this room?"

They all nodded.

"Is this some kind of white slave market?"

The girl from Milan started crying. The girl next to her put her arms around her and cradled her.

"Shut up," she hissed at Cash.

"Well, damn, I just want to know what I'm dealing with." Cash sat back down on the bed, the springs creaking. She looked toward the window again. Saw the top of the cathedral. Her Ranchero was down there on the street. It couldn't be that far away. And her .22 was behind the seat. For a brief moment she lost herself in a daydream of the .22 in her hands, shooting through the door and running down the stairs. The other girls running after her. *Well, that's not going to happen*, she thought.

"How many other people are in this house?" she asked.

One of the girls held up five fingers. Another one pointed as if straight through the wall and held up four fingers.

"There's more girls here?" Cash asked.

They all nodded.

Cash sat and thought about that for a bit.

"Who are these guys?" she asked.

Again, all of them looked at the door.

"Speed freaks, I think," one of them finally whispered. "Sometimes they smoke marijuana, but mostly they're skinny and scrawny and jumpy. Sometimes they give us little white pills that keep us awake for hours."

"Or black capsules."

"Are they making you sell yourselves for sex?"

The Milan girl started crying and shaking. The girl holding her held her tighter and shushed her, glaring at Cash.

Cash shrugged. "I only just asked."

"Not her," the girl said.

"Not yet," said another of the girls.

The Milan girl started gulping, holding in her wails, but her body shook uncontrollably.

Cash lit another cigarette. This time just tapping the ashes directly onto her jean leg.

Cash heard a couple sets of footsteps coming up the stairs.

All five girls froze. A key turned in the lock.

Two tall, very thin white guys stepped through the open door. Their long hair was greasy. Their faces unshaven. "Come on, chippies. Bathroom and food break. Grab your cans."

The girls teetered upward on their high heels, moving en masse toward the open door, each of them with a Folgers can. Cash stood to follow.

"Not you, squaw. Sit back down. Gordie here will be back for you in a sec."

Cash felt the rage start in her belly and flow through her chest, then up through the base of her neck. As soon as the women were escorted out of the room and the door was locked behind them, Cash walked to the door and put her ear to the wood. She tried the handle. No luck. She heard all the steps go toward the bathroom, but the door never shut even as the toilet flushed five times. Cash heard the girls set their coffee cans down outside the door, then all the footsteps tromped down the stairs.

Cash searched the room, rifled through the clothes

in the closet—all of the garments were short and thin, sparkly or psychedelic. The makeup was for white faces and the lipstick bright red or fuchsia pink. The sheets on the bed needed washing and the flat, gray-stained pillows didn't have pillowcases.

Cash tried the window again. It still wouldn't budge. Now that she could take a longer look, she could see there was nothing outside the window but a straight drop down from the second floor. The house next door was a good bit away with no lights on in any of the windows. *Think, Cash, think.*

She heard men's footsteps coming up the stairs. She moved quickly away from the window, standing at the foot of the bed she had been sleeping on.

When the door opened, it was a different man than the two who had taken the girls. This must be Gordie. He was thin too, though not as tall as the other two. His teeth were tobacco-stained, odd to see in a guy who was probably still in his twenties. His hair was just as scraggly as the others, but he was wearing a braided leather headband.

"Well, lookee here, the old man got us a squaw." He looked her up and down. Walked between the two beds so he could view her from the side. Cash stood still. "Wow. Look at that hair." He pulled her braid. "No titties though," he said, flicking her chest. "Have to get you some falsies." His laugh was cruel. His eyes absent of humanity. They reminded Cash of the feral cats she had seen on numerous farms. "Do you talk? No?" He made some war-whoop noises with the palm of his hand over his mouth. Laughed again like a maniac.

Cash knew her eyes had turned black with hatred. She looked quickly at the wall in front of her instead of at him. It was "the look" that had gotten her beaten many times in foster homes. She had learned to look away, not engage, look down, shield the look with her eyelids.

He grabbed her chin. "What's the matter, don't you like me?" He pushed her backward onto the bed. "Yep, you and me going to have a little fun," he said as he unbuckled his belt and the top button of his jeans.

He leaned over her on the bed and shoved his left forearm over her chest, pinning her down. As she was gasping for breath, he stood up, quickly unbuttoned her jeans and pulled them and her panties off in one full grab, then spread her legs.

Cash felt her entire being go cold. It started in the pit of her stomach and rose to her eyes. She became cold with icy hatred. He pushed his forearm over her chest again as he unzipped himself and dropped his jeans farther down on his hips. Cash felt his hard penis brushing up her bare leg as he tried to get himself into position to penetrate her.

She looked at him, in his inhuman eyes, and in a calm, still quiet voice stated, "I imagine you don't take too long. Guys like you rarely do."

She felt his penis go limp against her leg.

She saw the rage build in his eyes. His forearm was still across her chest. He used it to lift himself up and slap her full force across her face. He stumbled to standing, pulling his jeans up over his limp dick, then lifted her by her shirt and backhanded her again. "Bitch. Squaw. Whore."

Inside her icy cocoon, Cash barely felt the blows. She had been here before. She knew that a beating always ended. She knew how to endure. He screamed and punched and spewed spit on her face. His greasy hair flew in strands around his red face. Finally he threw her, still half-naked, back on to the bed and stormed out of the room, slamming the door behind him, locking it as forcefully as a skeleton key could turn in a lock.

She got up and pulled her underwear and jeans back on. She couldn't find her shoes. Couldn't remember if she had ever had them in this room. She sat on the edge of the mattress and held her head in her hands. She breathed shallowly. She had gotten into bar scraps in recent years, but no one had beaten her since the night Wheaton had rescued her from the last foster home. When he had found her sitting in the middle of a wheat field, in a truck used for hauling grain, contemplating slitting her wrists after a similar attack by the foster dad, Wheaton had rescued her. He had taken her from that home, set her up in the apartment she still lived in, telling some lie to the landlord about her being his niece or daughter who was ready to be emancipated and wouldn't cause any trouble whatsoever.

Cash didn't know how long she sat there. Reliving past beatings. Reliving past aches and pains that eventually healed. Finally, she stood up and walked over to the vanity mirror. Her braid was a tangled mess. Her cheeks swollen where he had hit her. She felt her face and nose. Nothing was broken. Her ribs hurt, and she was sore as hell. She found some water in one of the glasses and emptied the glass.

She could use a beer. She rummaged around on the vanity and found a half-smoked cigarette. She didn't know where her pack had gone. She lit up and took a big drag. The nicotine hit her lungs and calmed her nerves a tiny bit.

Shortly after, she heard a girl scream. A long, tortured piercing scream. It tightened all the muscles in Cash's belly. Cash took another deep drag on the cigarette. The smoke was stale coming from the last half of the butt, but it comforted her nonetheless. She tiptoed over to the wood door and pressed her ear against it. At first she pressed so hard all she could hear was her own heart pounding in her ear. She moved her head a fraction and was able to hear the muffled sounds of girls crying. One of the girls, whose cries bordered on screams, was clearly hurt. Men's voices were interspersed with harsh laughter. There was an acrid smell that drifted up the stairs combined with the smell of marijuana Cash recognized since it seemed to be the smoke of choice for her brother. Cash backed away from the door and sat down on the vanity. She dug around and found a whole cigarette, menthol, but she was beyond having a preference.

She lit up and looked around the room, a little bit at a time. It was big. Cash estimated it at around twelve by fourteen feet, with hardwood floors and lots of dark woodwork. One large front window, covered with a flimsy lace curtain, faced the street.

Another window, narrower, faced the house next door. The wallpaper was old—a creamy yellow with tiny red roses running from floor to ceiling. An eight-light brass chandelier hung from the middle of the ceiling. Three of the lights were burnt out. The closet was big enough for someone to lie down in, but it was strewn with clothes, with a few lonely ones hung on wire coat hangers. The rest of the room held a six-drawer dresser and two double beds. A vanity and bench. Each bed had a fitted sheet, a top sheet and a threadbare blanket. Rumpled on top of each was also some kind of tufted bedspread.

None of the clothes looked winter-ready. The four-inch heels were certainly not made to run in. Cash had no idea how many men were in the house. She had seen three, but the girls said there were five. *Think, Cash, think.*

She got up and walked softly to the window that faced the house next door. That house seemed to be exactly like the one she was in. If it was, there was another window right below the one she was looking out of. The window in front of her had a thick wood frame, with a top and bottom ledge that was a good four inches wide.

Cash was getting out of here. Period. No question

about it. One way or the other, she was getting out of here.

She pondered for a moment why the other girls stayed. Glass was breakable. Why had they not made a run for it? Then her mind shut down. Years of dead ends and no escapes had taught her not to ponder situations too much. The words from a poem she learned in freshman English ran through her head, "Ours is not to reason why, ours is but to do or die."

Damn, she was not going to die today.

She sat back down on the bed, cringing when the bedsprings creaked. No one came storming up the stairs. The acrid smell had drifted on, but the smell of marijuana was getting thicker. Cash grabbed a slippery scarf off the vanity and wrapped it around her mouth and nose. She wanted a clear head to deal with this situation. After a few minutes of thought, she got up and dug through the vanity drawers. No scissors. No knives. No other weapons.

Ha, a fingernail clipper. And the metal file was intact!

Cash pulled a top sheet off one of the beds. While well worn, it was strong cotton. She measured a hand width across the bottom of the sheet and clipped the material. *Rrrrippp.*

Bottom to top. She measured and clipped, ripped again. She shoved the strips under the chenille spread on the other bed.

When she finished with one sheet, she tiptoed to the door and listened. The crying had stopped. Just the low murmur of men's voices.

She went back to the bed and began tying the sheet strips together. She kept the strips under the spread, hidden, in case the other women returned, pulling out just the ends she was tying together. She used a bowknot she had learned from some farmer who had hired her to help him build a tree house for his kids a few years back.

When all the strips were tied together, she stepped into the closet and went way to the back, hiding the rope under the clothes scattered there. She measured the sheet rope along her body by stepping on one end and raising it the length of her body. She estimated two rope lengths were about ten feet. Altogether, she figured she had about thirty feet of rope.

She knelt in the closet and added another knot every four feet to give the girls a better handhold for the climb down. Even then, she figured it was still long enough to reach from the upstairs window where she was to about the middle of the window downstairs. If need be, it would be a short drop. Harmless. When she was finished, she walked out of the closet, the rope a big bundle in her arms. She stuffed it under the mattress at the head of the bed that was closest to the side window.

She dug around on the bed until she found the pack of Marlboros that must have fallen out when the ape had attacked her. She shivered, a quick body spasm that came up from the base of her spine and down her arms. As fast as the shiver happened, she clipped him—and what he intended to do—out of her mind.

She lit the cigarette and sat down on the mattress. She had no idea what time it was. Her internal clock seemed to have gotten messed up by whatever drug LeRoy had given her. Damned if she would ever get in someone else's car again. Or take a drink that she hadn't poured herself. She felt rage build and settle in the pit of her stomach.

She flicked the ashes from her cigarette directly onto the floor. She smashed the butt out with her foot and immediately lit another cigarette. She walked again to the side window where she could see the house next door. It had a front porch that covered the whole front of the building. The porch was built up a good three to four feet off the ground with wooden steps leading up to it.

Cash remembered the dream she'd had, a dream with a house like the one next door with the number 175 on it. If the house she was currently in was 175, then the lattice around the base of this porch had a tear in it, like in her dream. That porch on the house next door was large enough to hide five skinny girls under it. So this one should be able to also.

She got out the metal file from the fingernail clippers and began to scrape at the window caulking from around the glass in the window. She left just enough caulking so the glass didn't fall out and swept the caulk off the windowsill and put it under the pillow on the bed.

She heard the clomp of footsteps coming up the stairs and moved away to the vanity bench. The door opened and the five other girls came tumbling in. Way more disheveled than they'd left. Hair a mess, makeup smeared. The Tweed girl, with the help of another girl, half-carried a girl. Her eye makeup ran down and mixed with the splotches of lipstick on her face. Her eyes were dull and her skin was ashen. When the two girls laid her on the bed, her skirt rode up and Cash saw blistered skin—a crude brand. That had been the acrid smell. Burnt flesh. An ugly wing and star brand. Cash averted her eyes from the men at the door. Her hatred would blaze, and she had no wish to further antagonize them. She was leaving. So were these girls. One way or the other.

Without looking, Cash knew there were three men in the doorway. They smelled of oily hair and marijuana. Cash looked at them sideways from under her lashes. They were stoned. Moronic grins on their faces as they slid Folgers cans in across the floor. They backed out, pulled the door shut after themselves and locked the women in.

Without a word, Cash handed cigarettes to all the women. Held the match while they inhaled to light them. She brushed the hair off the forehead of the girl on the bed. "What's your name?"

One of the other girls answered, "Carla."

"Well, Carla, I'm getting you out of here. Tonight. Hear me? I'm taking you home, all right?"

The other girls started murmuring no's and huddling like scared chickens. Cash glared at them, the rage in her eyes not leaving room for questions or resistance. "We are leaving. Tonight."

She looked at the Tweed girl and said, "And you're helping me." Janet nodded.

"Finish your cigarettes and then we're going. We gotta move fast and gotta work together. Got it?" Janet and Carla nodded. The other three looked scared out of their minds.

"You don't want to stay, do you?" They all shook their heads no.

"Then you're gonna do what I say and we're gonna work together. Janet, get Carla over by the side window. The rest of you, get those clothes out of the closet and spread them across the floor in front of the door. No noise." Janet picked Carla up and moved her quietly. The other women, shoes off, began piling clothes in front of the bedroom door. Cash separated them into piles of four. She whispered, "One girl on each side of this bed. We're going to pick it up and set it on these piles of clothes in front of the door. Quietly."

The girls worked as a team. Lifting. Setting. Piling up more clothes. Silently. Then moving the other bed, sideways, ever so quietly between the first bed and the wall. There was no way that door was going to open. The only sound heard in the room was the occasional squeak of the bedsprings as the girls moved from one side of the bed to the other until they were all standing on a patch of dust-covered floor where the second bed had been. They looked at Cash with fearful determination, ready for the next order.

Cash looked at the lot of them. Half-dressed, skinnier than normal, terrified. All blond, all blue-eyed. They could have been a cheerleading squad. With a little more muscle. A little more wool instead of sequins and nylon.

Cash pointed to the girl who had helped Janet carry Carla into the room. Speaking softly, so the girls all had to lean in to hear, "You are going to go first." She pulled the makeshift rope out from under the mattress and tied it around the leg of the bed closest to the side window, yanking the bowknot to make sure it was secure. She removed the remaining caulk from around the window and slid the glass out, grabbing it quickly so it wouldn't fall. She lifted it up, pulled it out, leaned it against the bedroom wall. The cold night breeze drifted in. She used the metal nail file to cut the screen wide open.

There was nothing between them and freedom except fear and a thirty-foot drop. "This rope should be long enough to get you down so that if you do have to drop you're not going to break anything. The side of the house is brick, so you might be able to use the dents in the bricks as toeholds if you need to. Just get down as fast as you can and run to the side of the porch where the wood lattice is already partly ripped off. Crawl under the porch and be ready to help Carla get in there. Carla, you are going next."

The girl, still lying on the floor, looked at her wide-eyed.

Cash asked, "You want out?"

The girl nodded.

"Then you're going to climb out this window and run. Then crawl under the porch where she'll be waiting for you. Got it?" The girl nodded again. "Then one after the other we go. You get under that porch and you stay there, understand? I don't care how many men come out of this house screaming for you. Once you're under the porch they're not going to look for you there. They're going to assume you took off running. Understand? So stay there. Quiet. I'll come last. I'm not coming under the porch. I have a truck over by the Cathedral. I'm going to run get that and pull up front. I'll honk once, then you all haul ass and jump into the back of the truck."

They looked at each other, scared, hopeful, determined.

"Come to think of it, I'll honk as soon as I am on this block. You guys come running. Okay? Help Carla."

They all nodded. Cash lowered the string of sheets out the window. She looked out and judged that each girl might have a short drop once they hit the end of the rope but not enough to kill them.

Cash had never been a cheerleader, but she knew the pep routine. She knelt down and put her arm out. Carla was the first to put her hand on top of Cash's. The other girls knelt down and did the same. Cash mouthed the words, "Rah rah boom!" while pumping their hands up and down. Then she pointed at the first girl and mouthed, "*Go!*"

The girl backed out the window, feet first, hands gripping the rope so tightly her knuckles turned white. Cash whispered, "Find a toehold in the bricks and go! Quietly." The girl nodded and disappeared. Cash leaned out the window. When she was about halfway down, Cash pulled back in and said, "Your turn, Carla."

Carla stood, shaking. Cash could see the remnants of cheerleader muscles in the girl's thighs. "Wait till I give you the go. We have to make sure she's hit the ground."

The girl took a deep breath, closed her eyes and exhaled. When Cash said softly, "Go," she opened her eyes and crawled out the window. She winced once as she pulled the branded leg off the windowsill and then she was gone. Cash pointed at the other three. Silently numbering, one, two, three. The Tweed girl last. She was the biggest of the girls, the tallest, and she probably still weighed the most even after all she had been through.

One by one, each girl dropped into the night. As the Tweed girl descended, Cash ran to the vanity and grabbed everything she could fit in her arms. She began to throw hairspray cans, bottles, jars and hairbrushes at the bedroom door, making as much noise as she could as she made her way back to the window. She took hold of the rope, lowered herself out and down the side of the house, the palms of her hands burning because she opted to slide down the makeshift rope rather than go down hand over hand. As she dropped to the ground, she slapped her hands against her jeans to dull the sting and took off running. From above, she heard men hollering and pounding the bedroom door.

Cash hadn't even thought about being barefoot until the cold of the sidewalk numbed her feet. But by that time her head was a long way from her toes and she ignored them and kept running. As she turned the corner onto Selby Avenue, which she remembered was the street the Cathedral was on, she glanced up and read Western Avenue: 175 Western Avenue.

She was out of breath and had a side ache by the time she got to the Ranchero. Ignoring it, she dug into her jeans pocket and found the truck key. She had the truck unlocked, door open, her butt on the seat, engine running and gears shifted before you could say *Jack Sprat could eat no fat*. She barreled down Selby Avenue.

She screamed a long list of swear words at Professor LeRoy, at her own stupidity and the world in general. She banged the dashboard until her fist hurt. *Damn*! *Damn*! *Damn*!

She turned onto Western.

Just as she careened down the street toward 175 Western, she saw three men pushing themselves out the front door, looking wildly to the left and right. Hollering, shoving and pushing each other, not one of them directing the search. Cash whipped around the corner.

Damn, now what was the plan? She had thought those wackos would spend more time trying to get into the bedroom. *Damn.* She slowed the Ranchero and lit a cigarette, turned off the headlights and crept around the block.

When she came around again, she saw someone staggering down the street, singing off-key at the top of his lungs, "I'm going home, my tour is done. I'm going home, I'm a lucky one . . ."

"Son of a bitch . . . how the hell did he get here?"

Cash pulled to the curb. Her brother stumbled toward the three men coming down the porch. He hollered out at them, "At ease soldiers, atten-hut!" and gave them a sloppy salute. He stood on the end of the sidewalk, swaying, looking at them. They stared back at him.

"Did you see some chicks running that way?" one of them finally asked.

Mo looked back from the way he had come. "Nah, man, I woulda noticed some chicks. I'm a little drunk, but I ain't that messed up. I woulda noticed some chicks. You all missing some chicks? I wouldn't lose my chicks if I had some chicks."

He started swaying more heavily. Fumbled around for the pocket on his fatigue jacket and pulled out a pack of cigarettes and a lighter. After a few misses, he lit the dangling cigarette with his Zippo. "You all wouldn't happen to have some smack, would you? No? What about some grass? Or juice? Sure could use some juice. Got some juice you'd share with a brother?"

"Move it along, Chief," one of the men finally snarled, stepping down onto the first step of the porch.

"Get down the street and see if you can see the chicks," he snapped at the man right behind him. "They can't have gone too damn far."

The other guy stepped in front of him and headed across the grass. When he got within four or five feet of Mo, Mo slithered forward, smooth, like a snake striking. Even though he was much shorter than the other man, Mo chopped the guy in the throat with such force he sank to the ground.

Without breaking the fluidity of his movement, Mo whipped his punji stick out from the back waistband of his pants and struck the first guy square in the forehead using the stick like a short bat. The guy toppled over. The third guy was already running back into the house. Mo followed.

Cash honked the horn one short blast, turned the truck lights on and rolled toward the porch. Leaning out the truck window, she yelled, "Come on. Come on."

The Tweed girl was the first to crawl out. She turned and yanked Carla out from under the porch, pulled her to standing and pushed her in the direction of the truck. Carla crawled into the Ranchero's front seat, while the other three girls jumped into the truck bed.

Just as the Tweed girl hoisted herself up and over the tailgate, Mo came running out of the house hollering, "Di di mau, di di mau!"

He threw himself into the truck bed as Cash shifted gears and tore off down the street. In her rearview mirror, she saw a man come running out of the house waving a handgun, looking stupidly in either direction, not sure which way to give chase.

His buddies on the ground were just starting to come around. Cash turned right on Selby Avenue and lost sight of them.

A few blocks later, Mo leaned into the driver's window by stretching around from the back of the cab—scaring the crap out of Cash—and hollered in her left ear, "We gotta turn around, my car's back by that big ol' church you were praying at."

The last thing Cash wanted to do was go back where men with guns were looking for them. She thought about the .22 behind the driver's seat, but she wasn't ready for a shootout either. All she wanted was to get out of Dodge. Instead, she turned left and another left on a street named Laurel and headed back in the direction they had just come from.

A tap on her left shoulder caused her to jump and hit the gas. Mo told her to turn left again. The cathedral was right in front of them. She slowed down. Mo jumped out and ran up the street. He motioned for her to hold it.

In her rearview, she saw heads peek up from the truck bed. Carla rolled down her window and told them to stay down, everything was okay. Cash reached behind the front seat and pulled out her extra clothes and wool blanket. She passed them to Carla who passed the meager coverings to the girls in back. She reached down to the floorboard on the passenger side, felt around for her cowboy boots and pulled them on to her freezing feet.

It seemed like ages, but soon Mo's gray Grand Am was idling across the intersection ahead of them. He led them down a slight hill, out of downtown, and didn't stop until they had left the Cities far behind. Light from the still-hidden sun brightened the horizon behind them. Finally he pulled off into a farmer's plowed cornfield.

He walked back to Cash's Ranchero, grinning from ear to ear. "Not bad for a rookie," he threw at her.

Cash jumped out of the cab. "Where the hell did you come from?"

"Powers of deduction and incredible tracking skills," Mo said, tapping his right temple.

They walked over to his car and leaned against the trunk, looking back at the Ranchero, the girls watching them.

"Two more guys were in the house. Took them down in a second. Kicked down the door where some other girls were. I didn't stop to see who made it out."

Cash nodded. "I think we should keep driving until the stores start to open, then we can stop and get them some warmer clothes. I've got some cash in the car."

"It's at least another three, four hours to Fargo–Moorhead. Do you think any of them would want to ride with me? My car's got a heater."

Cash walked back and asked the girls. No. They all shook their heads furiously.

She shook her head no as she walked back to the Grand Am.

"Can't blame 'em." He turned around and used the car key to open his trunk. "Here, give them the sleeping bag. You got enough gas to keep driving?"

She did.

"Are we bringing them all to Fargo?"

"Yes . . . no, we'll go to Wheaton's first. In Ada. He'll know what to do."

"This is the most fun I've had in-country." He

swaggered back to the driver's door. "Let's rock and roll then, soldier."

The Tweed girl leaned out of the truck bed. "Are you taking us home?"

Cash nodded, tossed the sleeping bag to them. "Here, this will help cut the wind chill a bit. We're going to stop once the stores open, and my brother will go in and get you all some sweatpants, sweatshirts. A couple more blankets. Something to keep you warmer."

Mo came walking back with a six-pack of Schlitz in his hands. He set it in the back of the truck and started back to his car. About five feet away, like an afterthought, he turned and tossed a church key to the girls. It clinked as it hit metal. He kept going to his car, got in, started the engine and headed back out to the black top, his tires kicking up field dust. Cash jumped in the truck and followed. In the rearview mirror she saw the girls, huddled against the back of the cab, the sleeping bag wrapped around them all, pop open a beer. One of the girls tapped on Carla's window, then handed one up to her. Carla looked at Cash, asking with her eyes, *Do you want one?* Cash wanted to drink the whole six-pack but shook her head no.

The sun came up behind them as they caravanned

west, the sky a burst of orange and red. They headed toward Ada, to Wheaton. Using the wad of cash from under the car seat, they stopped once to buy sweat-shirts and sweatpants for the girls and to get hot coffee and homemade doughnuts. The girls pulled the sweat-pants and sweatshirts over their skimpy clothes. Mo had even bought a bag of athletic socks. They looked like a worn-out cheerleading squad.

The ride was a silent one, Carla deep in thought or sleeping, and the girls in back, after finishing the beer and coffee, huddled under the Army-green sleeping bag. They slept too.

When they reached the outskirts of Ada, Mo dropped back, signaling for Cash to take the lead to Wheaton's house. As the Ranchero slowed through the town streets, the girls all shifted awake, fear once again in their eyes as they looked around the town. The Tweed girl, once she realized they were in Ada, pulled her blanket up around her face, presumably hiding, in case anyone recognized her, though no one was out in the residential area of the small county seat.

Cash pulled to the curb in front of Wheaton's house. His car wasn't there. She parked and walked up the sidewalk anyway. She tried the front door. It was open. She motioned for the girls to come in. Warily, they climbed out of the truck and followed her into Wheaton's small, bare, tidy house. Cash directed them to the couch and easy chair in the living room, but instead they pulled out chairs around the kitchen table and sat down.

Cash stepped outside where Mo was waiting in the front yard, smoking a filterless cigarette, looking up at the few wisps of white clouds that floated across the blue sky. He lit one off the tip of his and handed it to Cash. She inhaled, then spit tobacco out of her tongue.

"Can you drive to the courthouse? Wheaton should be there. Tell him we need him over here?"

"Sure thing. Just point me in the right direction."

Cash went back into the house. She dug around in Wheaton's cupboards and found some Folgers and made a pot of coffee on the stove. She also found a couple cans of Campbell's Chicken Soup and heated them up too. Another foray into the cupboards found enough bowls for the girls and some spoons. All mismatched.

The girls were just finishing their bowls of soup, Cash leaning against the kitchen counter, when Wheaton and Mo walked back in, Gunner on Wheaton's heels. The dog, sensing the mood, went to each girl, nudging a leg until petted. Then he went and lay down on a rug in front of Wheaton's TV in the living room.

Wheaton took off his hat, shock and disbelief on his face. He looked at Cash. Worry filled his eyes. "Well, I'll be damned. You okay?" he asked. Cash sensed a whole lot of different meanings behind that question, but she nodded and waved her hand at the girls sitting around the table.

Mo excused himself for a cigarette outside. Cash wanted to follow him. Instead, she introduced Wheaton to the girls as her friend, even though he stood before them in his sheriff's uniform.

The only question he asked was, "Can I get your names and parents' phone numbers?" He opened a drawer and pulled out a small spiral notebook and pencil. "If you can write it down here, I'll call your folks."

They passed the notebook around the table and then back to Wheaton. He moved into his living room and sat in the easy chair. The girls in the kitchen could hear the *click-click* whirr of the telephone as he dialed their numbers.

One by one, he called them in by their first names, the Tweed girl first. Wheaton stood up and let them sit in his easy chair to use the phone. Each girl sobbed her way through the first contact with her mom and dad. Wheaton wrote down his address for the girls to give to their parents so they could come get them. All of the girls were from Minnesota, except one girl from Rugby, North Dakota, way up on the Canadian border. Cash hadn't questioned the girls, so she knew nothing of how each had ended up in the Cities except for the Tweed girl and the one from Milan.

Cash took a cup of coffee out to Mo and stood in the yard with him, smoking. Neither said a word. Cash went back inside. The girls were all in the living room, some still crying, others talking softly to each other, drinking more coffee. Wheaton was standing in the kitchen.

He spoke softly. "I'm going to have to call the feds about the girl from Rugby. Taking someone across state lines is federal. It will take her folks the longest to get here. The rest are all on their way. I'm going to interview them here. Get the key details. I've called my secretary to come over from the jail and type up our notes as we talk. She's pretty fast—I think she can get it all. I don't want to keep them here any longer than we have to. I already called the sheriff in Moorhead too. He's going over now to pick up that professor. He seems to be the one who was orchestrating this. I need more help than just me. This crosses state lines, counties, cities."

He swiped his hand through his crew cut.

"How did he manage to get all these girls?" Cash asked.

"He's from New York. Seems that's where he started getting young girls into prostitution. He works as a teacher so folks trust him. Once he moved here, he just kept doing it, found a market for girls in the Cities. He spent a lot of time in the Cities. No one questioned his frequent trips for conferences and state award ceremonies. He drugged the Tweed girl at the football game. She was going to go with some girlfriends to the Cities, but he separated her from the group with some story and drugged her. The Milan girl—he caught her in the hallway at the Curtis Hotel where her school was staying. The kids were being kids, playing hide-and-seek in the hotel, and he convinced her it was safe to hide in his room. And the girls have been from all over the state, so no one's had a reason to focus their attention on him. Some of the girls will probably never be found."

That worried look came back in his eyes. "What the hell, Cash. You all right?"

"Yeah." Cash grabbed her cigarettes off the counter and walked back outside.

Wheaton's secretary showed up and the clack of typewriter keys followed by the swish of the carriage was heard throughout the rest of the day. The Tweed girl's parents were the first to arrive. There was a lot of crying all day by everyone except Cash, Mo and Wheaton.

Other county sheriffs arrived to take statements from the girls and their families. Other parents arrived, most with siblings in tow. Judging from the parents' and the girls' statements, all of them were achievers, if not overachievers. They had been open and friendly before this. They were the cheerleaders and home-coming attendants, secure that they were the elite of their small town. Nothing had prepared them for their unfortunate trip to the Cities. It was beyond their knowledge, beyond their comprehension that such a sordid world existed or that they would be thrown and trapped in it. Favored in family and in school, nothing had prepared them to be hurt by men who had no regard for their innocence. Preyed on that innocence, in fact.

Cash had experienced firsthand people who had no regard for anyone else, people who wanted to destroy, out of some perverse sense, the light that shone in others. She smoked cigarette after cigarette, drank coffee after coffee to still the rage she felt building in her belly and chest throughout the day as she witnessed parents arriving to comfort, love and bring their stolen daughters home. Home—where they would be nurtured and loved back to wholeness as best they could.

At some point in the late afternoon, Wheaton asked Mo to run downtown and rent two hotel rooms. Two families had arrived after dusk and their daughters still needed to be interviewed.

When Wheaton's house was empty, Cash and Mo drove back to Fargo in separate cars. Without consulting each other, they both drove directly to the Casbah. Cash lifted two fingers at Shorty behind the bar as she entered. He put two Buds on the counter, opened them. Mo asked for two Schlitzes. As always, there was a game happening at the pool table already. Both Mo and Cash put up quarters. They slid into an open booth and drank their beers in silence. They drank, getting quieter and quieter as the night wore on, playing partners against whoever put quarters up.

Near closing time, some farm kid, drunk on his own beer and "white is right" attitude, called Mo "chief" one too many times. Mo punched him square in the jaw and knocked him flat out. He fell with a *thud* on the hardwood floor, chalk dust puffing up around him as he landed, no words exchanged at all. Cash grabbed her house cue by the narrow end, ready to use the handle as a club. By the time she had moved around the table to Mo's side, Shorty was also there, white bar rag in his hand. He looked Cash in the eye and said, "Take it outside, Cash. Take it outside. Now."

Though their cars were parked out front, Cash chose to exit by the back door. She went by Ol' Man Willie, who was passed out in his home booth. Cash picked up his half-empty beer glass and dumped it on his head, then threw it against the wooden wall in the booth, shattering glass all over him.

Outside she gulped air. Mo slapped her back. "Fuck 'em if they can't take a joke."

He took off running down the back alley, tipping over garbage cans as he went. Cash followed, pushing her pace to keep up. They ran until Mo stopped, bent over, gasping for breath. Cash doubled over too, sucking in air, holding her sides.

Mo grabbed some beer bottles that had fallen out of the last tipped-over trashcan. He flung the bottle with all his might at the second-story window of whatever business they were behind. He missed. Cash grabbed one and threw it with all her might. Closer. They continued throwing whatever hard objects they could find until Mo lucked out and shattered the glass above them. They ran to get away from the falling shards, slowing to a walking pace as they exited the alleyway. They turned down the sidewalk back toward the Casbah.

"I'm gonna go drive around," Mo said. "Catch you later."

Cash went back to her apartment and drank all the beer in the fridge, chain-smoking. At some point, she passed out, fully dressed on her bed.

She awoke the next morning to a disheveled Mo, cooking eggs and bacon, a hot cup of coffee ready for her. She went to the bathroom, opened the medicine cabinet and popped two aspirin. Ate her breakfast. Went back into the bathroom and took a quick bath to wash the drunk off. Clean, with hair brushed into one long braid and even her teeth brushed, she pulled on her zip-up sweatshirt, then her jean jacket.

"School?"

"Nah, Ada."

"Later, gator."

"How did you find us?" she asked, hand on the doorknob.

"You left me some notes on your dresser." He grinned, pointed at his temple. "My excellent powers of deduction and unparalleled tracking skills."

Cash pulled the door shut.

She was a couple of steps down when Mo popped his head out, the grin still on his face.

"What'd I tell you? White slavery."

Cash filled up the Ranchero at the Standard Station on the edge of Moorhead and then drove to Ada. She went by Wheaton's house, but no one was there, so she went to the jail.

His secretary was back at her usual seat, clacking away on notes. Wheaton was sitting with the Rugby family, the young girl tightly sandwiched between them. A couple of other men in black business suits were in the room also. Feds.

Cash got a cup of coffee and sat on her wooden bench in the reception area. It was "her" bench because it was where Wheaton had let her sleep the first night they met. Her mother had ended up in this jail after rolling her car in a ditch with her three kids in it. After that, her mother disappeared. And so did Mo. And her sister Chi-chi.

But now Mo was back. Her sister wasn't and neither was her mom. But the bench was hers. And familiar.

The oak seat was worn smooth from the countless number of folks who had sat right where she was sitting. The countless number of folks who had told their stories to the secretary, with her graying hair and tight-bodiced, homemade, below-the-knee dresses. The countless folks, freed from jail on bond or having served their time, waiting for their ride home. The wood warmed quickly to whatever body was occupying it.

Cash leaned forward, elbows on her knees, sipping her coffee, lulled by the men's voices in the other room, the occasional sentence from the daughter or mother, but mostly the men asking questions, receiving a soft answer from the girl, then the men repeating the answer out loud to each other, as if confirming the details. The *clack* of the typewriter kept time with it all.

Cash lost track of time. Occasionally, she would lean back and smoke a cigarette, dropping the ashes in the tall tin ashtray at the end of the bench. She was leaning forward, elbows again on knees, when she saw the shiny polished black shoes of the feds walk by, then the work boots of the dad from Rugby followed by his daughter still in the athletic socks Mo had given the girls. The stout dress heels worn by her mother came last. Cash didn't look up until she recognized Wheaton's worn steel-toed boots standing in front of her with Gunner's furry feet next to his.

"Come on," he said. "Let's go for a drive."

They drove west, toward the small town of Halstad on the banks of the Red River.

He stopped at Arnie's bar in Halstad and left Cash and Gunner waiting in the cruiser with the engine running. Gunner looked at Cash sitting there in the front seat like he was saying, "What are you doing in my spot?"

Cash rubbed his ears. "I was here first," she said, not meeting his eyes but looking out the passenger window.

Wheaton came out of the bar with two open Coca-Cola bottles and a pack of Marlboros he tossed in Cash's lap. He handed Cash one of the bottles of Coke and headed west, out of town toward the Red River. Once he got close to the river, he left the paved road and drove north on farm roads, a trail of dust kicked up behind them, following them.

After a while, Wheaton said, "Why don't you tell me what happened."

So Cash told him about the missing girls, the award—which was real, she really had won an award, she assured him—getting drugged by LeRoy and finding herself in the house with the other girls. She left out the part of the guy and the bed and shrunken dick. She told him about the girl getting branded. She told him about the rope made out of sheets and all of them climbing down the wall. About Mo showing up. "And then we all drove back home," she ended.

He drove in silence for another five miles, his hands clenched, knuckles white on the steering wheel. "Did anyone touch you? Are you okay?"

Cash turned her face to the car window, plowed fields moving slowly by, tears welled in her eyes. "I'm fine," she said. "I got us out before anything could happen to me. I'm fine. Really."

She willed the feelings out of her body and eyes. She turned, looked directly at Wheaton, a sheepish grin on her face, "I scraped my knee on the bricks going down the side of the house, and I think I have a smidge of rope burn from sliding down instead of going down hand over hand. That's it."

Wheaton harrumphed, pulled into a field and turned the car around, heading back the way they had come. He rubbed his hand over his crew cut. Rubbed his face, forehead down to his chin and stretched the skin. He looked her over, as if assessing any damage. "Okay," he finally said. "I told the feds I would interview you and write up a report. This is the interview. One question they have is why didn't you go to the cops down in the Cities?"

"Those guys had guns. All we thought about was getting the hell out of there. Going to the cops never even entered my mind. The girls just wanted to get home. I didn't think about cops until I thought maybe we should talk to you."

"Hmm. Might have to ask you a few more questions later on. Dot the i's and cross the t's. The feds and I will do the best we can to keep you and Mo's names out of this. No need to complicate things, okay?" He kept to the gravel roads even as they drove south along the river.

"And Mo? What about Mo?"

So Cash told him about Mo showing up at her door. About how his adoptive family had kicked him out and given the farm to their "real" son. How he had a gray Grand Am. She told him about the night of the punji stick flashback. And how the punji stick had saved them from the guys coming out of the house down in the Cities. How he was a better pool shooter than she was, which, yes, was hard to admit. And, yes, school was going fine as far as she knew. Her grades were good. Once they were back to her Ranchero she would give him her award to keep, if he wanted it.

While she was talking, Wheaton had left the gravel farm roads that snaked along the river and driven on the pavement heading north. When they reached the small town of Hendrum, he pulled into a parking spot in front of the town's café. As they exited, he told Gunner to guard the car. The dog lay down on the driver's side, ears perked up. All business.

Inside Wheaton ordered hot roast beef sandwiches for both of them and two cups of coffee. They ate in silence. Then he ordered two slices of blueberry pie, with ice cream. After the waitress cleared their dinner plates and they were waiting for their pie, Wheaton said, "Tell me again about this brother of yours."

So Cash repeated the story of waking up to the "shave and a haircut" knock. Mo standing at the door. Moving in. His story of his adopted family and their cruel behavior toward him after they'd adopted him, then thrown him out. At that part of the story, Wheaton put down his fork, his blueberry pie ignored while he stared out the café's window. The occasional car or pickup drove by. The elderly couple four booths down ate their meal in silence. The clink and scrape of their silverware on their plates was loud. From the kitchen Cash could hear a radio without being able to make out the words of the songs being played.

Wheaton didn't say anything for a long time. Cash was afraid he was going to ask her if she was okay again. She used her finger to scrape up some of the melted ice cream from her plate.

Wheaton finally turned back to the table. He looked Cash in the eyes and said, "That happened to me."

Cash's finger, dripping with ice cream, stopped mid-air on the way to her mouth.

"What?"

"My mom was Cree from Canada. Came down to work the fields like everyone else. No one ever told me much. She got pregnant. Never said who the dad was. Had me. The story they told me is that she was young. She left me with the family that raised me, legally adopted me. As their own. This was up on the North Dakota side of the river. Up by Grand Forks. I was their oldest son. They had a couple more kids. One of them a son. My younger brother and two sisters. I watched over them. Protected them from scraps at school. Did their homework for them sometimes."

Cash couldn't remember Wheaton ever putting so

many sentences together at once talking about himself. She stopped eating or moving. Afraid if he noticed her, he would quit.

"Worked the farm alongside the old man. Combining. Hauling hay bales. Milking the cows. I was captain of the football team. By the time I was in high school, it was like everyone forgot I was the abandoned Indian baby from Canada. Graduated high school. Joined the Marines and got sent to Korea. It was a short stint, to my way of thinking.

"But everything changed when I got back. That first Sunday afternoon, the old man said, 'Let's go check on the old homestead.' We got into his pickup. The old homestead was on the North 40. He parked and just sat there looking at the weather-beaten remains of his parents' house. Finally, he cleared his throat and said, 'You know, Dave'—did you know my first name is Dave?"

Cash shook her head no.

"He said, 'You know, Dave, we've been talking as a family while you been gone. About what's fair and it's the only thing that really is fair, Jacob being my son and all. Well, he's going to be the one to take over the farm.'

"I got out of the truck. Looked 360 degrees all

around me. Land that I had been working since I was knee-high to a grasshopper. It was a hot summer day. But I got cold. Ice cold, like I used to get back in Korea when we were getting shot at. Or when we were shooting at someone. I was scared of what I might do so I walked up to the old farmhouse. Stood around, looking at land that I loved and plowed and planted and sometimes cursed. Smoked a cigarette. Walked back to the truck.

"The old man started the engine and drove us back to the main farmstead. I went into the house and packed my duffle. Didn't take anything that was theirs, or that they had given me. Except the pickup. I went out and got into his pickup and drove off. The old man didn't even try to stop me. For about a week, every time I passed a cop car I thought I'd get pulled over for stealing. My payment for all those years of work was a fifteen-year-old pickup. His son is now one of the richest landowners up that way."

Cash's chest was constricted. "What did you do?"

"Went a bit crazy. Saw the countryside. Saw America first, before it was the thing to do. But this is the country I know. This Valley. This river. This flat land that goes on forever. The dang wind chill every winter. The wind blowing across this prairie we bend over and walk into. We get used to it. It becomes us. You know, when they sing, 'amber waves of grain,' that tugs at my heart. Still. Those are our wheat fields, Cash, our country. Our land, our birthright that they're singing about."

Cash picked up her fork and ate the crust of her blueberry pie.

"So they can just take us in and throw us out?"

"Happens more than we want to know. There are Indian kids, just like you, just like your brother, heck just like me, all over this Valley. Fostered out, adopted out, working their fingers to the bone—heck, many of them not being properly fed so they are nothing but muscle and bone to begin with, thinking that if they just do good enough, maybe, just maybe, someday they will actually belong.

"Mostly what I see is once they've been used up—in some cases broken beyond repair—they're thrown away like all the battered farm equipment you see sitting in the back of farmyards, back by the windbreak."

Wheaton finished his pie and held up his cup for the waitress to refill. "Anyway, I eventually came back and got the job I got. I like it. Suits me. You, you're going to finish school. Maybe you'll be a lawyer. You're

too smart to be stuck driving grain truck all your life.
Maybe get married, have a couple kids."

Cash sputtered on her coffee.

Wheaton laughed. "All right, maybe just law school
then."

"Maybe just a college-educated cop." They sat in
silence for a spell. Cash emptied her coffee cup and
put her hand over it when the waitress headed over.
Wheaton pulled some bills out of his pocket and laid
them on the table.

Dusk was starting to settle over the Valley. He drove
Cash back to her Ranchero and they did the farmer
hand wave over their steering wheels as they backed
their vehicles out and headed in different directions,
Wheaton to cruise around town, Cash back to Fargo–
Moorhead.

Out of habit she stopped by the Casbah. Mo wasn't
there like she'd expected him to be. She waved away
the beers Shorty held up to her and left as soon as she
entered.

She knew even before she reached the top step
leading into her apartment that Mo would be gone.
There was a note on the table. "Hey, soldier. I decided
to re-up. Don't worry, only the good die young. Catch
you on the rebound." His corner by the wall was bare,

his deck of cards sitting square on the table. Cash didn't touch the note. She turned and left the apartment and headed straight back to the Casbah.

CASH'S LIFE RETURNED TO THE routine she cherished. With beet-hauling season over, she did odd jobs and errands for the farmers she knew, either early in the morning before school or right after her last class each day. It kept some cash in her pockets in addition to what she won in her nightly pool games. She went back to shooting partners with Jim and his occasional late-night visits to her apartment resumed.

The Valley had its first snowfall, then the second and third. The dirt fields acquired their winter cover and the farmers put snow tires on their vehicles. Football season ended and basketball season began. She got one letter from Vietnam. The envelope was edged with red and blue slanted squares. Instead of a stamp, it was marked FREE in the upper right corner. Via Airmail was stamped below the FREE. Mo wrote about jungle rot and joked about white slavery. He signed it, *Don't Worry, Only the Good Die Young.*

On campus there had been a bit of gossip, students going silent and looking at her side-eyed as she walked by. But that died down quickly as pot, protests and finals took their attention.

Professor Danielson caught her in the social studies building one afternoon.

"Renee, Renee," he said. "I just wanted you to know, I had no idea, none at all. I'm sorry. I want to apologize for all of us here." Waving his hand around the hallway.

Cash looked at him, arms hugging her books tightly to her abdomen. In front of her she saw a middle-aged white man, not that different from the farmers she had grown up with. But the one in front of her, his muscles were slack and his shoulders rounded forward a tiny bit, from hunched-over reading, not from carrying heavy loads of cow feed or hay bales. In her mind she thought, *He's a creep, but a harmless creep.*

Cash ignored his apology and instead said, "The important thing is that all the men responsible, including Leroy, have been arrested and every single captured girl is now back home," then walked off.

Mrs. Kills Horses had chased her across the campus one day, shouting questions after her as Cash walked away, throwing yes and no answers over her shoulder. She outdistanced the guidance counselor, attempting to run in high-heeled cowgirl boots, her denim skirt flapping around her thighs. Cash avoided her office and didn't return to the Indian students' meetings.

Sharon, as always, wanted to know every detail of what happened. She followed Cash around, even started to get better at pool as she took every opportunity to question Cash. Cash's answers were brief, five words at best, made quickly before she bent over the table and took her own shot, shooting balls into the pockets, one right after the other.

Sharon did give up her quest of Danielson, claiming she was "disgusted with all men, except Chaské *and* there were things to be said for monogamy," a word Cash had to look up.

The Tweed girl didn't return to campus. Wheaton told Cash that the Tweed family had decided she would commute back and forth to the new Ag Tech school in Crookston. Her dad drove her in the morning. Her mom picked her up at the end of the day. She seemed to be doing fine, he told her.

It was the end of the semester. Cash was at the student union, practicing her cut shots between classes, aiming at the 9-ball when out of the corner of her eye she saw Tezhi, Bunk and Marlene enter. They headed straight for her table. She kept shooting. They each grabbed a cue stick. Tezhi said, "Me and Bunk against you and Marlene."

"Rack 'em up," responded Cash, stepping back from the table. "You go ahead and break first."

Tezhi was almost as good as Cash. Bunk and Marlene were probably better shots with a few beers in them.

Bunk said, "We're having an Indian students'

powwow the weekend after finals. AIM is coming up. Bringing some speakers and musicians."

That was the extent of the conversation during the whole game. Cash and Marlene won.

On their way out, Bunk said, pausing at the doorway, "Two weeks, Saturday night. There'll be a potluck at the usual place, then the powwow and speakers at the Newman Center across the street. See you." And they were gone.

Cash forgot the conversation. It wasn't until she was leaving campus after her psych final and saw a poster saying powwow and speakers at 7 P.M. that she remembered. The poster made her think of the night in St. Paul when she had sat in her car outside the AIM office and saw Long Braids get into the car with two women.

She decided to skip the powwow.

But when 7 P.M. Saturday rolled closer, she found herself pacing the small apartment. She folded and sorted her clothes. Opened and closed the fridge. Washed the small linoleum kitchen counter. Cleaned the bathtub. Finally, fed up with herself, she threw on a clean pair of jeans and T-shirt, redid her braid. She got on her hands and knees and pulled out her "go to town" cowboy boots. She grabbed her cue case, chucked it behind the car seat and drove to the Newman Center.

She sat in the Ranchero for half an hour, smoking. Her heart beat so fast she could feel it. "What the heck am I afraid of ?" she asked herself. She watched whole families walk into the Center. They must be coming from nearby reservations because she had never seen so many Indians in Fargo–Moorhead at one time. There were a couple of men in brightly colored feather bustles standing outside the main door, smoking cigarettes. A gaggle of teen girls wearing fringe dance shawls giggled every time a teen boy entered the building. Each time the door opened, she could hear the drum and the men's ankle bells keeping time.

Then a rush of people came out at once. They stood around and smoked. Cash saw Tezhi and Bunk sharing a cig. Each of them had their long hair braided in two braids wrapped in strips of red cloth. It was a look Cash hadn't seen before. They were wearing bell-bottom jeans with a triangular red material insert at the hem that made the bell flare even wider. Marlene joined them wearing the same outfit. When the crowd was finished smoking and they all returned inside, Cash worked up enough courage to get out of the truck.

She slid inside the main door. The meeting room was lined with folding chairs occupied by powwow dancers, some with full regalia, others with just a shawl or maybe a feather bustle tied over blue jeans. She scanned the room left to right and back again. Looking for familiar faces.

A small clump of students stood at the front of the room, all with red-wrapped braids and big flared bell-bottoms with red inserts. Tezhi had on a ribbon shirt, the ribbons down his back and chest longer than his shoulder-length braids.

Mrs. Kills Horses was at the front of the room, speaking into a mic. She thanked everyone for coming and was "so thrilled to be a part of this momentous occasion: the first powwow ever on our college campus." She introduced a man whose name Cash didn't catch. He approached the mic, wearing the exact same attire as the students but the ribbons on his shirt were longer than Tezhi's.

As he started to speak, Cash continued her scan of the room. Another group of Indians stood off to the side of the man speaking. Cash froze. Long Braids was standing up there. A young woman stood next to him, looking up at him, a big smile on her face, clearly more interested in Long Braids than in the speaker. Cash looked around the room one more time, then got up and left the building.

She spun out of the parking spot, raced through Moorhead, finally slowed as she crossed the river into Fargo and pulled into a parking spot at the Casbah. A couple of beers and a few games of pool and her heartbeat was back to normal and her "could care less" attitude was back in place.

Shorty did a last call. Cash turned toward the bar and held up two fingers. He nodded, put the Buds on the counter for her. She lined up the cue ball with the 8 and pointed her cue at the side pocket where she was going to send it. She bent over, gazed until she was in the zone, and then softly tapped the cue. It drifted down the table, barely moving. The ball didn't even make a sound as it passed the 8-ball. The 8 dropped into the pocket, and the cue drifted another three inches.

"Rack 'em and weep," she said to the farmer who reached out to put his quarters in the table. She turned to the bar to retrieve her beers and walked straight into Long Braids. He was carrying her beers to her, her two in one hand, his two in the other.

She took a step back and looked up. "Partners?" he said.

Cash grabbed her beers and turned to the table.

"Sure. Got a partner?" she asked the farmer. He pointed at his wife sitting in the nearest booth. She swayed a little when she stood up to get a bar cue, but she actually made two balls before scratching. Cash and Long Braids kept the table for two more games before Shorty hollered out, "Drink 'em up. I'm gonna close it down."

Cash finished her beer in big gulps. Put on her jean jacket. Broke down her cue and put it in its case. Started to walk out of the bar.

"I'll come with you," said Long Braids.

She didn't get into the Ranchero. She needed the night air to clear her brain. The snow on the sidewalk crunched under their feet. She could see their breath with every exhale. Halfway to her apartment, Long Braids spoke. "I saw you standing at the back of the room at the powwow. When I looked up, you were gone."

Cash didn't answer. Kept walking. He put his arm across her shoulders and pulled her to him. He tipped her chin up and kissed her. Deep, with longing. "I missed you."

"Yeah," said Cash. She shut off the thoughts in her brain and walked silently with him back to her apartment. Once there, she pulled two Buds out of the fridge, opened them, handed him one and walked to the bed. He flicked the sheet hanging over the doorway as he passed under it and raised an eyebrow at her. Cash plumped a pillow up against the headboard, stripped and crawled into bed, taking her Bud and pack of cigarettes with her. She watched Long Braids undress and crawl into bed beside her. She looked at the sheet covering the doorway and began her story of Mo, her brother showing up. Then she told him about the white slavery escapade, leaving out the part where she herself almost got hurt.

Long Braids leaned against the pillow on his side of the bed, drinking his beer, listening. When she was done with as much of the story as she felt like telling, he leaned over and kissed her, his braids, still wrapped in red cloth, falling on her chest. They made love. Slowly and tenderly. They smoked a cigarette and drank another beer that Long Braids retrieved from the fridge. He turned out the lights. He told his story about traveling with AIM, the protests they had engaged in at different college campuses and a big one at a construction site for a nuclear power plant down by the Cities. They made love again. Told some more stories. Drank another beer. Smoked half a pack of cigarettes together. About 4:30, he looked at the clock on her dresser and said, "I should get back to where we're staying. Your school put us up in some motel on the edge of town."

He pulled Cash close, their bodies warm under the blankets. After a few minutes, Cash turned away from him to look out the bedroom window, the window Mo had climbed in after scaling the brick wall. Long Braids folded his body around her back and held her, brushing the strands of hair that had come loose from her long braid, brushing them softly back off her forehead.

"I gotta go," he said softly. "You're my main snag, right?"

When Cash didn't answer, he hugged her tighter. "Right?"

"Right," whispered Cash. She felt him get out of bed and heard him pull his clothes on. Heard him walk out of the bedroom and across the kitchen floor. Heard him take a leak in the bathroom. Felt him, more than heard him, lift the sheet over the doorway and look at her one more time. Felt him drop the sheet and go back across the kitchen floor and out the door. She lay without moving for a good five minutes. Then she got up, made sure the apartment door was locked, grabbed one last beer—drank half of it as she smoked another cigarette—then fell sound asleep.

For the first time ever that Cash could remember, she slept until the clock on her dresser said nine. She sat up and looked at the window. It was daylight outside. She rolled out of bed and ran bathwater. She wrapped a towel around her naked body and started a pot of coffee. Once it boiled, she shut off the burner to let it cool down a bit. She went back into the bathroom and slid into the tub. Three cigarettes later she got out, dried off and got dressed. She didn't look at herself in the mirror. She knew her eyes would be blank slates. She had seen those eyes too many times before.

She filled her Thermos with hot coffee and pulled on her jacket. She walked back to the Casbah to retrieve the Ranchero, then drove over to the Moorhead side of the river and headed north to Ada. The snow-covered fields flashed by as she drove. Even with a thin layer of gray clouds covering the sun and sky, the glare from the miles and miles of white reminded Cash of stories she had heard of early settlers going snow-blind. Or their wives going snow crazy in their isolated sod huts on the endless prairie.

She had never heard those kinds of stories about her own people who had for centuries lived with the vastness of the Valley, moving into the Valley in the warm season and back into the northern forests in the winter.

She parked on the street in front of Wheaton's house. She needed—really needed—to see his face, to see the certainty that was always there for her in his eyes. She gave a quick rap on the door and walked in. Gunner met her first, ears perked, stared at her with that "what are you doing here?" look in his dog eyes. Cash bent down and grabbed his ears. "I was here first, so get over it."

"What?" asked Wheaton coming out of his living room.

"Nothing."

Wheaton looked at her, then the dog. He went into the kitchen and asked, "Coffee?"

"Sure."

Another figure emerged from the living room. It was Geno Day Dodge from Red Lake. It was his dad, Tony O, who had been killed over by Halstad. Cash had helped Wheaton find his killers. When she had made the trip up to Red Lake to find his family, she had met all his kids. If she remembered right, Geno was the third in a line of seven. She nodded hello to him and looked at Wheaton. Her turn to raise eyebrows.

Wheaton handed her a cup of coffee and motioned at a chair by the kitchen table. Geno walked back into the living room where Cash could hear canned laughter erupting from the TV. Wheaton sat down at the table, tilted his head toward the living room and told Cash how Geno had showed up two days earlier. He'd remembered that Cash said her friend was the county sheriff in Ada. Apparently his older sister Mary Jane was taking care of the littlest one at their aunt's house. The second to youngest had been nabbed by social workers. Geno thought they were living at a foster home in Fertile or maybe Twin Valley. His older brother and the one a year younger than Geno had moved in with an uncle who lived on the other side of the Red Lake village. Geno didn't want to go to a foster home, so he hitchhiked to Ada and showed up at Wheaton's office, asking for Cash or a cop named Wheaton. He told Wheaton he was willing to do any work needed. Suggested maybe he could be janitor at the jail in exchange for a place to sleep and a meal a day.

"I didn't have the heart to turn him away. He's gonna sleep here. Maybe do a bit of cleaning at the jail. I told him he has to enroll in school on Monday. I'll figure out something to tell the principal."

Cash nodded in agreement. Drank her coffee. "I forgot to give this to you," she said as she placed her award from the Twin Cities on his kitchen table. The edges were a little furled and there was a small coffee stain on one corner. "It's been in my glove box. I keep forgetting to give it to you."

Wheaton read it. He looked at her and smiled, a smile that reached his eyes. "Good one," was all he said. It was enough—but not quite enough to fill the enormous void created by all of the losses she'd had during her short lifetime. But she kept those feelings from her eyes and grinned back at Wheaton.

She finished her coffee, said she had to get going. Before heading out the door, she stepped into the living room and nodded goodbye to Geno. He nodded back.

CASH HEADED WEST TOWARD THE Red River. Like a magnet, she was pulled to the field northwest of the town of Halstad where Tony O's body had been found. She parked on the road and got out of her truck. She stood on the edge of the road, looking at where Tony O had died, leaving a wife, who died shortly after him from a broken heart—although folks would say it was from drinking—leaving seven children. One who was way too young to have to decide between being sent to a foster home, moving into an already overcrowded relative's home or hitchhiking to a new life on a girl's statement that her friend was a cop. Cash walked back to her truck and leaned across the edge of the truck bed. Still looking across the field, at the cottonwood trees and oak that snaked along the river a few hundred yards away.

She looked down and saw the sleeping bag Mo had given the girls to wrap around themselves on the ride from the Cities to Ada. A thick, Army-green sleeping bag. The sight of it hurt Cash's heart. She had forgotten it was back there.

She climbed up into the truck bed, zipped the sleeping bag shut and crawled in. It was ice cold, but soon warmed up from her body heat. It smelled of cheap perfume from the girls, cigarette smoke from Mo—or was that the smell of pot? She burrowed down into the bag, closing the top around her head to keep her body warmth in.

And then she started to cry.

Deep wailing sobs of grief.

She remembered the last time she had seen her mom. She remembered all the times Wheaton had been the only person to show up at one of her school events. She remembered the note Mo left on her table when he re-upped. It was on her dresser with the one lone letter from him. She remembered Josie Day Dodge throwing a glass jar across her kitchen, the glass shattering, when she realized her husband, Tony O, was dead.

Cash wiped her nose on her jacket sleeve.

She heard Long Braids's voice saying, "You're my main snag, okay?"

Cash curled into a tighter ball and cried some more.

The top of the sleeping bag was cold and wet with tears and snot. Cash took a deep breath and stuck her head outside. The cold air hurt her lungs, but she crawled out of the sleeping bag, out of the back end of the truck, and threw the bag on the gravel road behind the Ranchero. She jumped into the cab of the truck. With fingers shaking from the cold, her whole body shivering, she turned the truck on and drove back and forth over the sleeping bag, screaming obscenities, screaming until she was exhausted and couldn't scream anymore.

She threw the truck in neutral with the brake on and lit a cigarette, swiping the heat knob to full blast.

She turned the rearview mirror so she could look at her face. Damn, her eyes were almost puffed shut from crying. Her hair pulled in thick strands out of the single braid. She smoothed her hair down as best she could. She got out and gathered up the tattered sleeping bag, threw it back into the bed of the truck, turned the truck around and drove without thinking.

She headed northeast. Up by Shelly and a small town everyone made fun of named Climax. Having spent her entire teen years working for farms in this area, there was no chance of her getting lost. She drove, smoked cigarettes, let her mind drift as aimlessly as her truck.

She pulled off to the side of the road once to drop her jeans, squat and pee. Damn, it was getting cold. She drove some more. Sometimes on paved county roads and sometimes on gravel farm roads.

She figured she was somewhere near Twin Valley when she saw a country church sitting all alone on the prairie. And in a small plot next to the church was a cemetery with a handful of marble headstones and a few wooden crosses. There was a mound of fresh dirt that caught her eye.

Snow and gravel crunched under her feet as she got out of the cab. It was a tiny grave. Not much more than three feet long. There were granite headstones marking off a larger area around the smaller grave.

Maybe it was a family plot. She walked closer reading names and dates.

A blast of freezing air stopped her in her tracks. She looked at the plot of graves she was standing in front of. A headstone for a Reverend John Steene stood next to one for his wife, Lillian. Their date of birth was followed by unblemished granite waiting for a date of death. Cash looked at the two other graves in the family plot. They were small graves, all with the last name Steene.

Cash read the dates of birth and the dates of death. She read them again, did the math in her head. Each was the grave of a child who had lived only two years. And the children had been born two years apart. The new grave didn't even have a headstone.

"What the hell," Cash said out loud, and a cloud of cold air swirled around her face.

AUTHOR'S NOTE

The National Crime Information Centre database reported that 2,758 Native women were missing or murdered in 2018. That number grows. As more Native women have disappeared or been murdered, our female relatives have created tribal, local and national platforms to call attention to this epidemic. In 2019, it is estimated that up to 4,000 Native American women are missing or were murdered in Canada. In the United States the number is estimated to be close to 3,000. First Nations people comprise only four percent of the total Canadian population. In the United States we are only one percent of the total population. Given those numbers, the high rate of missing and murdered Native women should be seen as a national tragedy.

The trafficking and murder of women and children, of all races, is a worldwide epidemic. *Girl Gone Missing* skirts around the edges of that story. Two true cases were the murders of Tina Fontaine (2014) and Savanah Greywind (2017). Both women were dumped in the Red River of the North—the river Cash, the fictional character of this book, crosses daily to go to school or work. In this story, I hope to honor all missing, murdered and unwanted women.

There is another backstory within this story. Following the boarding school era, there was a time in which Native children were removed from their homes and fostered into white homes. On a national level, an estimated twenty-five to thirty percent of Native children were taken and placed in non-Indian homes or institutions up through the mid-1960s. In Minnesota those numbers jump significantly. An estimated sixty percent of children were removed from Red Lake Reservation and between forty to sixty percent were removed from White Earth Reservation during this foster care era.

The Indian Adoption Project created by the Bureau of Indian Affairs occurred simultaneously. This federal program existed from 1941 to 1967 and allowed adoption agencies to systematically remove Native children from their birth parents. Eighty-five percent of them were placed in white adoptive homes. In the Southwest, this adoption process allowed Mormons to take thousands of Navajo children to work their farms. The Catholic Church and other Christian denominations took Native children from other tribes and placed them for adoption in non-native homes.

Because adoption records of these children were sealed, many lost their tribal identities and information that might lead them back to their families of origin. It is unknown how many Native youths faced the predicament that both Wheaton and Mo faced in *Girl Gone Missing*. This book is a work of fiction, yet this dis-inheriting of adopted tribal youth when they came of age is a common story throughout Indian country. It was one more way to "disappear" Native people from the national consciousness. It is my hope that you, reader, will search farther for the truths once you have read this story. It is my hope that you also see how generous Cash is in her rescue of girls who are different from her. I hope you see the resilience that inhabits us as Native people.

Miigwetch.

ACKNOWLEDGMENTS

So many people have made this writing gig possible. The "Women from the Center" writing group. Always—Danny, Eileen, Jeanne and Liz, Diego. All the folks who read *Murder on the Red River* and then asked, "How is Cash doing? What is she doing?" Questions that made me sit down and attempt to give you an answer. Lee Byrd for a painless editing experience. My children and grandchildren who continue to tolerate the absolute silence I require to write—no TV, radio, Netflix, YouTube. They live in techno-cultural deprivation so I can write. And of course, ALL the women in my life who have helped with children, food and emotional sustenance, you are in my heart forever. Chi miigwetch to you all.

ABOUT THE AUTHOR

Marcie R. Rendon is a citizen of the White Earth Nation. Her novel *Murder on the Red River* won the National Pinckley Women's Debut Crime Novel Award, 2018. It was a Western Writers of America Spur Award Finalist 2018 in the Contemporary Novel category and it was translated into German and Italian. Marcie has written two nonfiction children's books: *Powwow Summer* (Minnesota Historical Press) and *Farmer's Market: Families Working Together* (CarolRhoda). She was recognized as a 50-over-50 Change-maker by AARP Minnesota and POLLEN, 2018. With four published plays, she is the creative mind of Raving Native Theater. She curates community-created performance and stages Native scripts. Diego Vazquez and Rendon received the Loft's 2017 Spoken Word Immersion Fellowship for their work with women incarcerated in county jails.

Most importantly, Rendon is a mother and grandmother.

Continue reading for a peak at the next
Cash Blackbear Mystery

SINISTER
GRAVES

Cash sat in a battered fishing boat on murky flood-water that was headed to the Red River. The spring flood covered the Valley as far to the east and west as she could see. Schools closed. No one could get to church to pray. The prehistoric, glacial Lake Agassiz existed once again. What had been plowed fields of wheat and corn, soybeans and oats, potatoes and sugar beets was now an ice-cold, snow-melt lake as far as the eye could see. Sixty miles wide from one side of the valley to the other.

Cash took a break from oaring, removed a mitten and dipped her hand in the frigid water. If you got caught in the floodwaters, the freezing temperatures would kill you as fast, or faster, than the rushing water. She quickly pulled her hand back out and cupped it near her mouth as she blew warm air over her fingers. Even bundled up in a winter jacket, scarf, mittens and a stocking cap pulled low over her ears, she still shivered in the cold.

Al, a friend of a friend of one of the regular drinkers at the Casbah bar, was sitting in the rear of the boat. Cash carefully turned around on the seat, so she was facing him. He wasn't bad-looking. His hair wasn't as long as a hippie's but not a short farmer buzz either. His skin said Indian. Cash guessed to herself he was a veteran from Vietnam.

As Al navigated the floodwaters he would either drop the small motor into the water to move them along faster or bring the motor up when the water was too shallow. At that point he would oar the boat with her.

Just a week ago the Red River Valley had been snow-covered. It had been a long winter with whiteout snowstorms that left four-foot road drifts and piles of snow taller than the haystacks in the fields. Then there was one day warm enough for snowmelt. That's all it took—one day in the valley at forty degrees, followed by three more days with temperatures that didn't drop below freezing. The Wild Rice River, with its head-waters on the far eastern shore of the ancient Lake Agassiz, carried the snowmelt down into the Valley. And when the Wild Rice, along with a hundred other small tributaries, rapidly flooded their banks, all the water moved in a murky rush to spill across the fields of the Valley, the farms and towns, to join the muddy red snake that ran to the north.

Farmers had scrambled to sandbag their barns to keep their cows safe before moving to bag their own homes. Then they rode tractors into town to fill more bags to lay around the perimeters of the small towns; the huge tractor tires kept their bodies safe above the floodwaters.

Cash had spent eleven hours the day before throwing sandbags with a chain of humans—one end of the chain filled bags with sand, then ten to fifteen people passed the full bags to those at the end of the line, who then laid the sandbags like bricks to create a dike in order to keep the river from flooding down-town Fargo. It was a rush against the forces of nature.

It happened almost every year with the snowmelt. The only questions ever asked were how high would the water rise and how long would it stay. This year was one for the records. Water rose and rose. It overflowed the riverbanks, filled the fields, crept into barns and homes, and the streets of the towns that didn't sandbag fast enough. The floodwaters covered the land from the Red River Valley to Lake Winnipeg way up north in Manitoba. Farmers prayed for the water to recede in days, not weeks.

When Cash arrived home after helping fill sandbags, she had been so bone-weary that she flopped into bed without getting undressed and didn't wake up until the incessant ringing of her landline woke her. No one except Wheaton ever called. What few friends she had, had given up on her ever answering her phone. Most just dropped by and hollered up to her apartment. Or made the journey up the flight of stairs and knocked. But that early morning phone call rang and rang. It stopped briefly, then started ringing again.

Cash finally pushed herself off the bed and stumbled to the kitchen, where the beige rotary phone sat on the counter. She picked up the handset. "Yeah?"

"Cash, it's Wheaton. What are you doing?"

"Sleeping. There's a flood out there."

Silence.

"What?"

"We have a body here that floated into town."

Silence.

"Where?"

"Ada."

"Highway 75 is flooded. I don't even know if I can get over to Moorhead. Last night they were saying the river might crest over the bridges in downtown."

"Maybe someone's got a boat that could get you out here."

More silence.

"You'd have to follow the road up. Stay away from the river. River's going too fast to try and get on. Maybe a boat with a motor could get you up Highway 75 or 9—9 might be safer. Water's not as deep and there really is no current. The water is just sitting on the fields, waiting for the river to empty up north."

Cash leaned her head against the counter. Her waist-length braid slid over one shoulder. Even though she worked out each week in the judo class at the university, the muscles in her arm holding the phone had been sore from moving sandbags all day. She pulled the headset away from her ear and stared at it.

"Cash?"

"Yeah. Okay." She hung up.

The phone rang again.

"Cash?"

"What?"

"You hung up. Are you coming?"

"I said okay." And she hung up again.

It had taken some doing and a promise of a twelve-pack, but she finally found someone—Al—to ferry her the forty-five miles north. The sky was overcast. The last thing the Valley needed was snow or rainfall. The clouds didn't look like they were ready to drop any more moisture, but they created a gray mass moving to the east above the muddy water moving to the west. A depressing, cold day no matter how you looked at it. Occasionally the small boat had to fight the moving current but, mostly, it was an easy ride traveling north.

Al navigated through the flood-filled ditch along Highway 9. The murky water was about a foot over the pavement but you could still see the white road lines. Al lifted the motor and he and Cash used the oars to bring the boat to land where floodwaters met the highway. Al, who was wearing wading boots, jumped out and pulled the boat up and out of the water. He tied it to a highway sign, and they walked the few blocks into town. Al to the local bar and Cash to the jail.

Wheaton, the county sheriff, was sitting at his desk. His dog, Gunner, lying at his feet. Gunner ignored

Cash's entrance. A few months back Wheaton had seen a gunny sack running down a gravel road, which ended up holding a small black mutt inside—probably a mix between a German shepherd and a Lab. Now, Wheaton and the dog were inseparable. Cash was certain the dog resented her presence in Wheaton's life.

Wheaton was eating half a roast beef sandwich. He held the uneaten half up in her direction. They ate in silence—her on the oak bench she considered hers and him at his desk. Back when she was three, Wheaton had pulled her family out of a ditch that her mother, who had had a few too many beers at the local bar, had rolled her car into. Cash had spent that night, and a few more, sleeping on the wooden bench she now sat on. Shortly after, she'd ended up in the foster care system. Wheaton had been the adult who stayed a constant in her life. Checking in on her, rescuing her again when things got really rough in the last foster home. He was the one who had gotten her the apartment in Fargo. Got her to enroll in college. Insisted she "make something of herself."

When he finished his sandwich, he handed her half his chocolate chip cookie. He called out to his secretary to bring them both a cup of coffee. Lots of sugar and cream.

As they sipped their coffee, Wheaton finally spoke. "There's a body over at the hospital. In the basement. Looks to be about thirty, maybe thirty-five. Maybe Indian. Kinda hard to tell. She floated in with the floodwaters. Some high school students who drove to the edge of town to watch the water come in found her. Thought if you came and got a look at her you might be able to tell me something."

Years ago, when Cash was in junior high, she had checked out a book from the bookmobile about meditation and yoga. Books were her escape from the world she lived in. There were days in the foster home where she was forced to sit in a chair with no food for the weekend. Bathroom breaks were scheduled three times a day. With nothing better to do, she practiced reading the minds of the people in the house. When she got bored with that, she practiced out-of-body travel and bending metal forks with her mind. She had discovered that mind-reading wasn't that hard and that out-of-body travel involved slipping out of her physical body and traveling through the air.

There were nights she dreamt she was an eagle gliding through the sky, looking down through rooftops, seeing what people were up to. Through these dream experiences she often knew things would happen before they happened in the physical world. Or she found out things she wasn't supposed to know. Her knowledge of one foster father having had an affair with a woman from the church had caused untold drama when Cash had casually let it slip one evening over dinner, saying, "*I had this crazy dream.*" Everyone went berserk, with her taking the worst beating.

After that, the next time she saw Wheaton at a school basketball game, she went up into the bleachers and sat by him. When he'd asked how things were going, she told him the dream, how she told the family and how everyone had freaked out. She told him that sometimes she knew things and then they would happen, they would come true. Wheaton just nodded and listened without comment. He was one person Cash could count on to not make her feel crazy.

A few months after that conversation, Cash dreamt about some boys from a neighboring town who stole a pickup and some gas from a farm way out in the country. Cash did not know that Wheaton was looking for whoever was stealing gas and vehicles from farmsteads throughout the county. When she told Wheaton her dream, she was surprised by all the details of the dream he wanted to know. Cash had said, "All I dreamt was the ringleader's first name, and that he's from Felton." Within a week, Wheaton had found the ringleader and his wannabe gang members. The main kid was sent to some state juvenile facility. Shortly after, Wheaton had asked her to share any other dreams or hunches with him she might have from then on.

After the foster father's affair drama, Cash learned not to discuss what she knew with anyone except Wheaton.

"What do you think?" Wheaton's question pulled her back into the current situation.

"Beats school. Or hauling sandbags."

Wheaton stood and pulled on his winter coat. "Stay," he said to Gunner. "Mind if we walk? We can get there faster than it will take for the heater to kick on in the car."

Cash hadn't bothered to take off her winter gear. "Let's go then." Her voice was muffled from behind the scarf she rewrapped around her neck and over her mouth.

They walked in silence the short couple blocks to the county hospital. Wheaton led the way into the basement, which served as the county morgue. Their footsteps down the stairs and across the marble floor echoed. Cash got chills as they stepped inside the heavy door that opened into the morgue. A body, covered with a white sheet, lay on a metal table in the middle of the room. The air smelled of formaldehyde and alcohol. Doc Felix sat on a metal stool pulled close to another metal table that was bolted to the concrete wall. Cash fought the urge to gag, not sure which repelled her more: the sight of Doc Felix or the sight of Doc Felix eating a chicken sandwich in the same room as a dead body.

In an earlier situation, she'd met Doc Felix when a dead man was found in a field northwest of town. At that time Doc Felix's breath had smelled of alcohol, and his disrespect toward the dead man, who was from the Red Lake Reservation to the north, had angered her. She had reckoned her feelings were justified by the way he looked her up and down with distaste.

He spoke to Wheaton. "S'pose you're here to see the waterlogged girl."

He walked to the table and unceremoniously pulled the sheet down to the dead woman's waist as she lay naked. He smirked at Cash as he did so. She ignored him.

She looked at the woman. Her long brown hair lay in ropey strands.

Doc Felix walked around the table inspecting the woman, side-eyeing Cash. "Kinda looks like you. Maybe a relative, huh? Then again, you all kind of look alike—hard to tell you apart sometimes."

"Quiet, Doc," said Wheaton. "What do you know about cause of death?"

"She didn't drown. No water in her lungs. If I had to guess, she took a few hits to the head. And then she was most likely smothered." He pointed to some lumps that were just visible under her hair.

"Someone beat her to death?"

"I think she probably got knocked out. Then smothered to finish the job."

Cash kept silent while the men talked. She walked slowly around the table. Doc Felix was right; the woman could have passed for Cash's relative, but Cash doubted it. The woman was lighter-skinned than Cash's year-round tan. Although that might be because she had been in the water. She was too young to be Cash's mother and too old to be Cash's sister, neither of whom Cash had seen in sixteen years. Cash shook her head, more to her thoughts than to anything either man in the room was saying.

She caught a glimpse of a thick, tall, dark shadow standing in the corner of the morgue. When she turned to look squarely at it, she heard a guttural *hmmph* and the shadow dissipated.

She looked back at Wheaton and Doc Felix, both of whom were standing and facing the direction the shadow had been in; neither showed any concern. Cash redid the scarf around her neck and tilted her head at Wheaton, signaling she was ready to leave.

As they started to walk away, Doc Felix said, "Don't you want to know what I found in one of her garments?"

They both turned back around.

Felix was smirking. "Sorry I didn't say anything right away. Slipped my mind." He walked over and opened a drawer in the steel table against the wall. "Found this in her bra. All folded up and wet. Been letting it dry out in the drawer. Looks like a page torn from a hymnal. One line's in English, the other in gibberish." He handed the damp piece of paper to Wheaton, who looked at it carefully before handing it to Cash.

Cash scanned the page. "*Asleep in Jesus! From which no one ever wakes to weep.*" The words of the song continued down the sheet between the musical notes. Underneath the English words were others written in Ojibwe, a language Cash would have known if she hadn't been separated from her family and raised in white foster homes.

An electric current ran from the paper to her hands, stinging her fingertips. She quickly handed it back to Wheaton and left the room. The swinging doors closed behind her with a swoosh. She was halfway up the stairs before Wheaton caught up with her.

Other Titles in the Soho Crime Series

STEPHANIE BARRON
(Jane Austen's England)
Jane and the Twelve Days
of Christmas
Jane and the Waterloo Map

F.H. BATACAN
(Philippines)
Smaller and Smaller Circles

JAMES R. BENN
(World War II Europe)
Billy Boyle
The First Wave
Blood Alone
Evil for Evil
Rag & Bone
A Mortal Terror
Death's Door
A Blind Goddess
The Rest Is Silence
The White Ghost
Blue Madonna
The Devouring
Solemn Graves
When Hell Struck Twelve
The Red Horse
Road of Bones

CARA BLACK
(Paris, France)
Murder in the Marais
Murder in Belleville
Murder in the Sentier
Murder in the Bastille
Murder in Clichy
Murder in Montmartre
Murder on the Ile Saint-Louis
Murder in the Rue de Paradis
Murder in the Latin Quarter
Murder in the Palais Royal
Murder in Passy
Murder at the Lanterne Rouge
Murder Below Montparnasse
Murder in Pigalle
Murder on the Champ de Mars
Murder on the Quai
Murder in Saint-Germain

CARA BLACK CONT.
Murder on the Left Bank
Murder in Bel-Air
Three Hours in Paris

HENRY CHANG
(Chinatown)
Chinatown Beat
Year of the Dog
Red Jade
Death Money
Lucky

BARBARA CLEVERLY
(England)
The Last Kashmiri Rose
Strange Images of Death
The Blood Royal
Not My Blood
A Spider in the Cup
Enter Pale Death
Diana's Altar

Fall of Angels
Invitation to Die

COLIN COTTERILL
(Laos)
The Coroner's Lunch
Thirty-Three Teeth
Disco for the Departed
Anarchy and Old Dogs
Curse of the Pogo Stick
The Merry Misogynist
Love Songs from a Shallow Grave
Slash and Burn
The Woman Who Wouldn't Die
Six and a Half Deadly Sins
I Shot the Buddha
The Rat Catchers' Olympics
Don't Eat Me
The Second Biggest Nothing
The Delightful Life of
a Suicide Pilot

GARRY DISHER
(Australia)
The Dragon Man
Kittyhawk Down

GARRY DISHER CONT.
Snapshot
Chain of Evidence
Blood Moon
Whispering Death
Signal Loss

Wyatt
Port Vila Blues
Fallout

Under the Cold Bright Lights

TERESA DOVALPAGE
(Cuba)
Death Comes in through
the Kitchen
Queen of Bones
Death under the Perseids

Death of a Telenovela Star
(A Novella)

DAVID DOWNING
(World War II Germany)
Zoo Station
Silesian Station
Stettin Station
Potsdam Station
Lehrter Station
Masaryk Station
Wedding Station

(World War I)
Jack of Spies
One Man's Flag
Lenin's Roller Coaster
The Dark Clouds Shining

Diary of a Dead Man on Leave

AGNETE FRIIS
(Denmark)
What My Body Remembers
The Summer of Ellen

TIMOTHY HALLINAN
(Thailand)
The Fear Artist
For the Dead
The Hot Countries

SEICHŌ MATSUMOTO
(Japan)
Inspector Imanishi Investigates

MAGDALEN NABB
(Italy)
Death of an Englishman
Death of a Dutchman
Death in Springtime
Death in Autumn
The Marshal and the Murderer
The Marshal and the Madwoman
The Marshal's Own Case
The Marshal Makes His Report
The Marshal at the Villa Torrini
Property of Blood
Some Bitter Taste
The Innocent
Vita Nuova
The Monster of Florence

FUMINORI NAKAMURA
(Japan)
The Thief
Evil and the Mask
Last Winter, We Parted
The Kingdom
The Boy in the Earth
Cult X
My Annihilation

STUART NEVILLE
(Northern Ireland)
The Ghosts of Belfast
Collusion
Stolen Souls
The Final Silence
Those We Left Behind
So Say the Fallen
The Traveller & Other Stories
House of Ashes

(Dublin)
Ratlines

KWEI QUARTEY
(Ghana)
Murder at Cape Three Points
Gold of Our Fathers
Death by His Grace

KWEI QUARTEY CONT.
The Missing American
Sleep Well, My Lady

QIU XIAOLONG
(China)
Death of a Red Heroine
A Loyal Character Dancer
When Red Is Black

MARCIE R. RENDON
(Minnesota's Red River Valley)
Murder on the Red River
Girl Gone Missing

JAMES SALLIS
(New Orleans)
The Long-Legged Fly
Moth
Black Hornet
Eye of the Cricket
Bluebottle
Ghost of a Flea

Sarah Jane

JOHN STRALEY
(Sitka, Alaska)
The Woman Who Married a Bear
The Curious Eat Themselves
The Music of What Happens
Death and the Language
  of Happiness
The Angels Will Not Care
Cold Water Burning
Baby's First Felony
So Far and Good

(Cold Storage, Alaska)
The Big Both Ways
Cold Storage, Alaska
What Is Time to a Pig?

AKIMITSU TAKAGI
(Japan)
The Tattoo Murder Case
Honeymoon to Nowhere
The Informer

CAMILLA TRINCHIERI
(Tuscany)
Murder in Chianti
The Bitter Taste of Murder

HELENE TURSTEN
(Sweden)
Detective Inspector Huss
The Torso
The Glass Devil
Night Rounds
The Golden Calf
The Fire Dance
The Beige Man
The Treacherous Net
Who Watcheth
Protected by the Shadows

Hunting Game
Winter Grave
Snowdrift

An Elderly Lady Is Up
  to No Good
An Elderly Lady Must Not
  Be Crossed

ILARIA TUTI
(Italy)
Flowers over the Inferno
The Sleeping Nymph

JANWILLEM VAN DE WETERING
(Holland)
Outsider in Amsterdam
Tumbleweed
The Corpse on the Dike
Death of a Hawker
The Japanese Corpse
The Blond Baboon
The Maine Massacre
The Mind-Murders
The Streetbird
The Rattle-Rat
Hard Rain
Just a Corpse at Twilight
Hollow-Eyed Angel
The Perfidious Parrot
The Sergeant's Cat:
  Collected Stories

JACQUELINE WINSPEAR
(1920s England)
Maisie Dobbs
Birds of a Feather